# Dare to Take

## THE DARE TO LOVE SERIES, BOOK #6

*New York Times* Bestselling Author

# CARLY PHILLIPS

SPENCER
**HILL**
PRESS

Dare to Take
Copyright © 2016 by Karen Drogin

Please visit www.carlyphillips.com

First Edition: 2016
Carly Phillips

Dare to Take: a novel / by Carly Phillips—1st ed.

Library of Congress Cataloging-in-Publication Data available upon request

Summary: There are some guys you just don't touch—even someone as inno-
cent and inexperienced as Ella Shaw knows that. But when her best friend's
brother is up for grabs and willing, she can't resist. After all, she's wanted
him for years . . .

On leave from the army, Tyler Dare is just looking for a little fun, but his
sister's best friend is off-limits. Yet, unable to deny how sexy and alluring she
is, he finds it all too easy to succumb to a night of passion and heat that ends
the next morning in the worst way possible.

Now Ella is stranded on a tropical island with a hurricane bearing down,
and only Tyler can save her. It's his chance to make amends for the past and
show the woman he's never forgotten that he's coming after her . . . in more
ways than one.

Published in the United States by Spencer Hill Press
This is a Spencer Hill Contemporary Romance.
Spencer Hill Contemporary is an imprint of Spencer Hill Press.
For more information on our titles visit www.spencerhillpress.com

Distributed by Midpoint Trade Books
www.midpointtrade.com

Cover design by: Sara Eirew
Interior layout by: Scribe Inc.

ISBN: 978-1-63392-088-0
Printed in the United States of America

# The Dare to Love Series and NY Dares Series

## Dare to Love Series

Book 1: *Dare to Love* (Ian & Riley)
Book 2: *Dare to Desire* (Alex & Madison)
Book 3: *Dare to Touch* (Olivia & Dylan)
Book 4: *Dare to Hold* (Scott & Meg)
Book 5: *Dare to Rock* (Avery & Grey)
Book 6: *Dare to Take* (Tyler & Ella)

## NY Dares Series

Book 1: *Dare to Surrender* (Gabe & Isabelle)
Book 2: *Dare to Submit* (Decklan & Amanda)
Book 3: *Dare to Seduce* (Max & Lucy)

The NY Dares books are more erotic/hotter books.

# CONTENTS

# Chapter One

he sun shone overhead, the temperature neared ninety, and the humidity was hair-curlingly high on the Caribbean island of St. Lucia, making it hard to believe a hurricane was coming soon. Ella Shaw glanced up at the blue sky, knowing it wouldn't remain pristine for long.

The calm before the storm.

She pulled her hair into a high ponytail and headed out of her hotel, determined to hit the local gift shop she'd caught sight of on her way to the photo shoot yesterday. She'd seen long, draping, blue-beaded necklaces from the storefront window, but she hadn't had time to stop. Her boss was a stickler for getting the right shot in the exact light, and they'd worked well past dark. By the time they'd wrapped for the day, the store had been closed.

As an assistant for Angie Crighton, a fashion designer based in Miami, Ella was responsible for the little details involved in a photo shoot. And though Angie, the photographer, and models had left the island this morning, Ella had stayed to make sure the shooting site was clean, the hotel pleased enough to allow them back another time. And if she were honest with herself, she liked the downtime after the craziness of a photo shoot, the rushing around of the crew, and the bossiness of some of the models and, of course, of Angie herself.

Ella appreciated the fact that she had time to souvenir shop for her best friend, Avery Dare. How ironic was it that the two girls from very different worlds had met at all? But they had. And it was Avery who'd introduced Ella to the finer things in life, leading her to seek out a job with an haute-couture designer. Whereas Avery came from a wealthy family, Ella had been raised firmly middle class, but the two girls had bonded instantly. They'd even shared an apartment until recently, when her best friend had moved in with her rock star fiancé, Grey Kingston.

Yep, two different worlds, even now, Ella thought wryly. But their friendship was solid. Which reminded her, she needed to let Avery know she might not make it back to the States tomorrow as planned.

When Ella had heard about the storm changing course, she'd tried to book an earlier flight out without success. She shivered at the possibility of being stranded here alone during a hurricane and knew Avery would like the news even less. Her best friend suffered from severe anxiety, and Ella didn't like to make her worry.

She'd just buy Avery an extra gift to make up for it, she thought, walking into the shop. She immediately headed to the turquoise-blue beads she'd seen through the window. The shopkeeper claimed they were Larimar beads. Even if they were fake, the beads, popular in the Caribbean, were said to have healing powers. Ella purchased two dozen, a mix of bracelets and necklaces, so she could share with the children at the cancer treatment center where she and Avery volunteered.

Avery had been nine and Ella ten years old when they'd met at a Miami hospital, both donating bone marrow, both there at the behest of a parent. Neither of them really understanding what was happening. All Ella had known was that she was doing a favor for her father, helping the stepmother Ella didn't like all that much to begin with. Even at a young age, Ella had been a good judge of character, a better one than her father, obviously, because shortly after Janice had gotten well, she'd left Ella's dad. And both her father and Ella's life had gone downhill from there. Ella shook off the thoughts of her past before she could go deeper and darker, and focused on the pretty jewelry.

She spent some time choosing a thick turquoise bracelet for Avery and a similar one for herself before paying for everything and waiting for the shopkeeper to wrap things up.

Bag in hand, she started back to the hotel, cutting through side streets and looking into the windows of the stores, soaking up the culture along the cobblestone streets before heading back to Miami tomorrow. At least, she still hoped she'd be home. Knowing she couldn't change the outcome, she pushed her worrisome thoughts aside. She'd deal with the situation as it came.

Sweat dampened her neck from the humidity of the island, and she contemplated taking a cab back to the hotel. She reached into her straw bag and pulled out her cell phone to make the call, when, without warning, she felt a hard jerk on her purse.

"What the—?" She spun around, but whoever wanted her purse was quicker.

She barely caught a glimpse of a tall guy with dark hair as he yanked harder, nearly pulling her shoulder out of its socket before slamming her against the nearby building with his other hand.

Her head hit the concrete wall, and spots immediately appeared behind her eyes from the impact. As she struggled not to pass out, the man grabbed her purse, along with her cell phone that had fallen to the ground.

She opened her mouth to scream, but nothing came out. Her legs collapsed beneath her, and she fell to the ground, her head smacking the sidewalk before everything went black.

Tyler Dare had a full day planned, a packed schedule of appointments with existing and potential clients of Double Down Security, the firm he now co-owned with his brother Scott. Serena

Gibson, his close friend and personal assistant, had strict orders not to let anyone interrupt him this morning so he could pull together his notes for each meeting.

He picked up the threat assessment sheet for his first client, a diplomat who needed protection for his family, and had begun to scan the findings when he heard raised voices.

"I'm sorry, Avery, but he said no interruptions," Serena insisted.

"That's okay, I'm sure he'll see me." His sister's voice carried through the closed office door.

"Avery, he said not to let anyone inside." Serena's voice rose, but he knew the soft-spoken woman was no match for a determined Dare female.

Sure enough, his door swung open, and Avery barreled inside, Serena a step behind her. "Sorry, Tyler."

He waved her worry away. "It's fine."

"Thank you, Serena," Avery said in a sweet voice. "I'll buy you coffee one day soon."

"Make it a martini and you're on," Serena muttered, heading back to her desk.

Tyler knew the other woman meant it. She was a single mom, raising her young daughter alone after her husband had . . . died. Tyler pushed thoughts of Jack Gibson to the far recesses of his mind. Going there meant reliving way too much pain. Pain he'd left behind him when he'd departed from the army.

Instead, he turned to his sister, and with a groan, he rose to his feet. "Couldn't you have called first? I'm swamped today. And what if I was in a meeting?"

Avery rolled her eyes . . . and why not? When she wanted to get her way, she did. She and Olivia, their sister, were typical Dares, stubborn and headstrong, just like him.

She strode over and placed both hands on his face, meeting his gaze. "Family comes first, isn't that what you always told me?"

A distinct edgy tingle raced up his spine. Quoting his words back at him meant she wanted something.

But she had a point. Ever since their father had announced he had another family, moved out, and divorced their mother, his oldest brother, Ian, along with Tyler and Scott, had circled around their sisters and mother. Nothing was more important than family. Even if Tyler still felt like he'd been a coconspirator in betraying them all, having walked in on his father and his mistress when he'd visited his dad at work a year before everyone's life had imploded.

His father had guilted him into keeping his secret. "You don't want to be responsible for your mother's pain, son. Be a man. Keep my secret."

As an adult, Tyler understood Robert Dare was responsible for everyone's pain. But as a kid, all he'd wanted to do was protect the mother he adored . . . and be a man, as his father had said.

All conflicting, fucked-up feelings for a kid to handle. So he hadn't handled it at all. He'd kept the old man's secrets, never admitting the truth, not even to Ian or Scott, and in doing so, he lived with the knowledge that, had he spoken up, he could have spared his mother the humiliation of how she'd found out. When his father had approached her with the painful demand that all her children be tested as bone marrow donors for one of his other kids. Because when things got emotionally difficult, Tyler ran. And that hadn't been the only time.

"Tyler, are you okay?" Avery asked, placing a hand on his arm.

"Fine." He shook off the past. "What's up?" he asked, focusing completely on what his sister wanted.

"It's about Ella."

His dick immediately perked up at the name. "Ella."

Avery narrowed those violet eyes in confusion. "Yes, Ella."

"Ella," he repeated, his brain flickering with images he'd long sought to expunge from memory. A lithe body with pert breasts, warm, silken skin covering his own.

"You know, Ella Shaw," his sister said, breaking into his memories. "My best friend."

And the woman whose virginity he'd taken when she was eighteen.

Yes, Tyler knew exactly who Ella was. It was just that every time he saw her face or heard her name, his brain short-circuited and a mixture of self-loathing and guilt threatened to crush him, followed immediately by a shock of arousal he had no right to feel.

"What's wrong with her?" Tyler asked, already turning his attention back to the day ahead, potential clients he wanted to acquire, new security systems he thought existing clients should agree to upgrade to.

Whatever issues Ella had, Tyler felt certain she didn't need him to handle them. Avery was overreacting. She had to be.

He made it a distinct point to keep as far from Ella Shaw as possible. It was better for both of them to pretend that night had never happened, and by silent, mutual agreement, they'd managed to keep that mistake from Avery.

Avery slammed her hands on his desk, bringing his focus back to the situation at hand. "Ella was mugged in the Caribbean. She's in the hospital with a concussion, her passport is gone, along with everything in her purse, and a hurricane is headed straight for St. Lucia."

Shit, shit, shit. "Is she okay?" he asked, more concerned than he wanted to admit.

"I don't know. She sounded groggy. The nurse wouldn't let her stay on the phone, but Ty, she can't leave the island without proper documents, and all her identification is gone. She can't get to the American Embassy since they won't release her from the hospital for another twenty-four hours because she's alone. And when she is released, the hurricane will have hit and—" Avery didn't get another word out because she started to hyperventilate.

Tyler recognized the signs. She'd been suffering from panic attacks since she was a kid, and though they were mostly under control now, truly stressful situations caused an attack.

"Come on. Sit." He wrapped an arm around her shoulders and led her to a chair, easing her down. "Do you have your

Xanax?" She nodded and, though still breathing fast, began to look through her purse.

"Serena, I need a glass of water, quick!" Tyler called out to his secretary.

She rushed in a few seconds later, a cup of water in hand.

"Thanks," he said.

Avery took the pill and began to do breathing exercises.

"Can I get you anything else?" Serena asked.

He shook his head, his focus on Avery. "We're good for now."

Serena quickly stepped out, shutting the door behind her.

"Okay, look," Tyler said, kneeling by his sister's side. "You're going to write down where she is, and I'll contact the embassy. I'll do what I can to get her out."

"You have to go yourself. Please. I need to know Ella is okay and with someone I trust after all she's been through." She grasped his hand and squeezed tight. "Ian will let you take his jet. Private is the only way she can fly out without a passport anyway."

She gazed up at him with the same big eyes he'd been a sucker for when she was a kid. Except this time she had no idea what she was asking of him, as the past came flooding back.

He'd come home on leave from the army just in time for Christmas. As usual, Ella had been visiting for the holiday. And holy shit, she was hot. Her body had filled out, with sexy tits and sweet curvy hips; she'd knocked him on his ass. For the first time, he'd seen her as a beautiful woman and not his little sister's best friend, and he'd had to remind himself many times over the course of the night she was off-limits.

Except nobody had given Ella the memo.

In hindsight, he should have seen she'd had a crush on him for years, but she'd just been the kid he looked out for, the little girl he'd met when she was donating bone marrow to her stepmom. He'd always felt protective of her, mostly because she was such a little thing for so long.

Once he'd enlisted, his trips home were sporadic, and he hadn't seen Ella in years. Not until that night.

"Tell me you're on fucking birth control," Tyler had said to a very naked, beautiful, and obviously vulnerable Ella. But he'd been too angry with himself and, at the time, with her, to see it.

She'd managed a nod, her brown hair hanging over her bare shoulder, her hazel eyes a damp mossy green. "I am."

Relief had flooded him. She might have crawled into his bed uninvited, but he'd known damn well what he was doing when he'd thrust inside her. She'd been so damned tight, and when he'd hit that obvious barrier, he'd realized immediately . . . but it was too late. His control had snapped, and he'd taken her hard and fast, nothing like what her first time should have been like—and would have, if he'd been sober. If he'd known she was a virgin. But if he hadn't been drunk, she wouldn't have made it into his bed in the first place.

"It's okay." She'd reached out and touched his bare chest, the sweet gesture a brand on his skin, and his body had woken up again, hardening for her. Which had only served to piss him off more.

"No, it isn't okay. It was a big fucking mistake. A mess, and you better believe it won't be happening again."

Tears had filled her eyes as she'd gathered her clothes, pulled her long shirt on, and had run, slamming his bedroom door behind her.

"Fuck." He'd fallen back against the pillows, so furious at himself he couldn't think straight.

Traveling to the Caribbean to rescue Ella would bring them alone together for the first time since he'd looked her in the eye and spoken with all the finesse of a drunk twenty-three-year-old.

He'd been an ass. Worse, he hadn't stuck around the next day to apologize. He'd kissed his mother good-bye and lied, saying he'd been called back to base, all to avoid facing Ella. And in the years since, he hadn't manned up any better. He ran a hand through his hair, now longer than regulation length. If any man had treated his sisters the way he'd treated Ella, Tyler would have had their balls.

"Ty? You'll go get her, right? What if it's worse than a concussion and they misdiagnosed her? She needs someone there before the storm hits."

He groaned, already having come to the same conclusion. "Yeah. She does." He grabbed a pen and paper from his desk and handed it to Avery. "Write down everything you know about where she's staying and what hospital she's in. I'll call Ian and have him get in touch with his pilot."

"Umm, plane's fueled and ready," she said, a flush staining her cheeks.

Tyler shook his head. "That sure of me, hmm?"

"You're a good guy, Tyler. Plus you're the best at what you do. If anyone can handle things for Ella, I know you can."

Oh man. Talk about more guilt. If Avery knew about his past with her best friend, she wouldn't be sending him down to take care of her. But he couldn't worry about what Avery would or wouldn't think. He had to make sure Ella was okay, and to do that, he needed to check the weather forecasts and hope like hell he could get onto the small island before the storm.

The flight had been bumpy, and by the time Tyler landed, the wind was whipping through the trees. His goal was to get Ella settled safely into the hotel before the hurricane hit. He arrived at the hospital to find pure chaos. Unlike an American-run place, with generators and general preparedness, the staff was more concerned with getting themselves home than with the welfare of their patients.

He stopped a few people before someone, finally, directed him to the American woman down the hall. Considering she'd been mugged, the fact that they didn't ask him for ID or worry that maybe he was out to hurt her concerned him. It made him all the more determined to get her out of there as soon as possible.

During the trip down, he hadn't stopped to ask himself why he was doing this. He'd said no to his sister before. Not often, but he managed when he wanted to. So why put himself in the position of rescuing a woman he had such a messy history with? One who surely wouldn't be happy to see him, and whom he'd have no choice but to apologize to?

And there he had his answer. He'd let her down, and she wasn't the first person in his life he'd disappointed when they needed him, and he was trying to make amends and correct his past mistakes.

Tyler, like all of his siblings, had idolized their father, Robert Dare. After his other life and family had come to light, he'd shattered each child in different ways.

Ian had stepped up and taken over as man of the house. Sure, Tyler and Scott had helped look after their sisters, but it was Ian who'd held them together. And by taking care of the family, Ian had made sure Scott could be a cop and Tyler could do what he wanted with his life.

And what had Tyler done? Instead of facing the anger he felt at his father, Tyler had run away, joining the army, telling himself it was a big FU to his dad. In reality, it was a cowardly act of betrayal to his family. And when he'd come home on leave and treated Ella so badly, had he faced her the next day? No, he thought, combing a hand through his hair. He'd run again.

He wasn't ready to delve back into how he'd learned these lessons courtesy of Jack Gibson, who'd bailed on his family, on life, in the worst possible way. Tyler visited that in his nightmares often enough. But learn them he had. And if Ella's mugging and the damned hurricane gave him the chance to make things right, he would. He owed her a lot more than an apology.

For the last nine years, he hadn't been able to get the night with Ella or the morning after out of his head. Now was his chance to make it up to her and get rid of some of the guilt he'd been carrying around for being a dick.

For calling her a mistake.

For a lot of things.

He walked down the hall and stopped outside the room he'd been directed to. He drew a deep breath and stepped inside.

Ella was asleep, her light-brown hair spread out over the white pillowcase, her face pale. Though she looked fragile, he knew she was strong. He admired her and had never stopped thinking about her over the years . . . as more than a family friend. As the woman he'd treated so badly . . . and the one he'd let get away. Not that there was anything he could or would do about that now. He still didn't trust his ability to commit. And Ella, with her painful past, needed someone who wouldn't bail on her again.

Seeing her in this bed brought him back to the time when they'd met. She'd been small for her age, a ten-year-old waiting to give bone marrow to her stepmother, much like Avery. Except Avery was giving her bone marrow to a half sister they'd known nothing about until a few weeks before.

Avery and Ella had bonded over their mutual situation, and all the Dare brothers had become extremely protective of Ella Shaw. It was what made his reaction to her that Christmas so damned . . . wrong. And why he'd treated her so badly afterward. Self-disgust turned at the wrong person. Because he'd enjoyed her hot, slick body too much.

He shook his head, pushing those thoughts aside.

He stepped farther into the room, and as he made his way toward her, those protective instincts he'd always had for her kicked in, combined with a healthy dose of desire for the woman lying helpless in the hospital bed.

"Excuse me. Who are you and what are you doing in here?" a female dressed in white, presumably a nurse, entered the room and asked.

"I'm here for Ella Shaw. I'm . . . family," he said, forcing out the words, because what he felt when he looked at her was anything but familial or brotherly.

The nurse narrowed her gaze. "Well, she's been through a trauma and—"

"It's okay, he can stay," Ella said, her voice raspy and low.

The nurse studied him for a long moment, finally treating him to a curt nod before rushing out of the room.

Tyler turned back to meet her gaze. "Hey, short stuff," he said, the nickname from when she was younger falling off his tongue.

"When I feel better, I am going to strangle Avery," she muttered. "I take it you're the cavalry?"

"You could sound more grateful."

"And you could speak to me like an adult," she snapped back, both falling into recent patterns.

To keep his distance and not show how attracted he was to her, he'd put up a wall, treating her like an annoyance or a pesky younger sister. That shit had to stop now. She was right. They were both adults, even if he hadn't been acting like one for the last few years.

He pulled up a chair, his knees touching the metal frame of the bed. "How are you?" he asked more gently.

She blew out a breath. "My head hurts badly, and I'm a little dizzy. Nothing out of the ordinary for a concussion," she said, eyes suspiciously damp, telling him she was in more pain than she let on.

Without overthinking, he reached for her hand. "I'm sure you'll feel better when we get you out of here."

"I was mugged. My money, passport . . . everything's gone."

"I know. But the good news is you don't need any of those things to fly out on a private jet."

The noise she made sounded more like a snort. An adorable snort but one nonetheless. "Of course not."

"Got a problem with that?"

"I wouldn't know. I've never flown that way before but . . . I'm grateful you came for me," she said, looking past him, toward the window, obviously unable to meet his gaze. "I'm sure you didn't want to and Avery had to twist your arm."

He squeezed her soft hand. "We'll talk about all that when you're stronger. Right now let's find a doctor who can release you."

It took a while. Finally, a harassed-looking man agreed she could leave as long as she had someone to watch over her. Since Tyler wasn't letting her out of his sight, that wouldn't be a problem.

The trip back to the hotel was more difficult, costing Tyler a fortune because, again, most cab drivers wanted to get home, not take passengers out of their way.

The palm trees swayed dangerously as they drove, the driver holding tight to the wheel of the small car.

Ella was oblivious. No sooner had he bundled her into the back of the cab than she'd curled up beside him, laid her head on his shoulder, and passed out. She might have been hospitalized, but she still smelled pure female. He hadn't thought anything could distract him from the fury of the hurricane, but one whiff of Ella's hair, an inhale of her scent, and he wasn't thinking about wind or rain. He was immersed in a force of nature of a whole different kind.

What kind of perv got an erection when a hurt, unconscious woman lay trustingly against him? Shit. The things this woman did to him always had him questioning his common sense.

When they reached the hotel, he woke her, and she leaned against him as they walked inside. He explained the situation to the desk clerk, who, thankfully, because of the photo shoot, remembered Ella and was willing to give her a key. With his hand on her back to steady her, they took the elevator up to the sixth floor, and she directed him to her room, 618, with a *Do Not Disturb* sign on the door.

"Wait, I didn't leave that on there," she said, pointing to the door hanger.

He narrowed his gaze. "Wait here."

He glanced around, but there was no safe alcove in which to hide her. He pushed her against the wall on the same side as the room in case someone came running out, then pulled out his gun.

Her eyes widened, but she didn't argue.

He slid the key into the door and let himself inside. The bathroom was immediately to the right, and he pushed open the door. Empty, as was the bathtub. The closet was on the left. He slid open the door. Also empty. He checked the balcony, which was still locked tight from the inside.

But the room had been ransacked, all her things tossed around. This unexpected turn of events told him the mugging probably hadn't been random. "Shit."

He stepped back only to find her waiting in the room, mouth open.

"Didn't I tell you to wait in the hall?" he asked, pissed she hadn't listened.

She frowned at him and stepped inside. "Why would someone do this?" she asked, taking in the mess.

"That is a damned good question."

She bent down to pick up a piece of clothing.

"Don't touch!" he barked out, harsher than he intended.

"What? Why not?" She rose slowly to her feet.

"So when the cops here investigate, at least they'll see things exactly how we found them." Although with the hurricane coming, Tyler doubted anyone would have time for or care about a burglary.

A glance at Ella, who was pale and shaky, and Tyler knew that he, on the other hand, cared a lot.

# Chapter Two

*E*lla barely stayed on her feet while Tyler reported the break-in to the front desk and insisted on a new room. If she'd had the strength, she'd think about the fact that the sexy man she'd wanted forever had come to her rescue and currently had an arm wrapped around her waist, holding her up. Preventing her from sliding to the floor with his sheer strength.

He also smelled so good she wanted to bury her face in the crook of his neck and inhale the masculine scent that always affected her so strongly. But all those things also meant she'd be forced to recall the reasons they barely spoke in the first place and that when they did, it was rarely pleasant. And Ella never wanted to go there again.

Never wanted to revisit her stupid mistake and greatest shame. But from the look in his eyes when he'd said they'd talk later, she had a feeling she wouldn't get her wish. So for now, all she wanted was to lie down and rest her pounding head.

"You're going to report this to the police, I assume?" Tyler asked the desk clerk, who was currently looking for an open room in which to place them.

Luckily a lot of people had fled St. Lucia in anticipation of the storm, so they could move to a room that hadn't been broken into. Another thing she'd focus on if her vision and mind weren't fuzzy.

"Of course, but you should know that all the island personnel are busy with the state of emergency due to the hurricane," the woman said, clicking away on what she claimed was a very slow-working computer. Also due to the storm.

"In other words, it may take a while," he muttered.

"I'm sorry. Here is your key," she said, sliding a card across the counter. "It's an inside room, no terrace. I figured with the winds, you would want as few windows as possible."

He nodded. "Thank you. Come on." Never letting Ella go, he steered her toward the bank of elevators across the hall.

A few minutes later, he opened the door to a new, freshly cleaned room. Without missing a beat, Ella crossed the floor, headed straight for the king-size bed, the only bed in the room, and crawled on top of the mattress with a loud groan.

She distantly heard Tyler pick up the phone and order food, though she couldn't imagine having the energy to eat.

She didn't remember or register anything else until the sound of a cell phone alarm penetrated her senses. She opened her eyes and found herself facing Tyler's bare, muscular chest. Her head rested on his forearm, and she was smothered in delicious, masculine warmth. Unable to resist, she took that inhale she'd been dreaming of earlier, and his musky scent sent tingles of awareness rippling through her veins.

Apparently a concussion didn't prevent desire from kicking in, because headache or no headache, her nipples pulled into hardened peaks, and slickness coated her panties. She couldn't imagine a more inappropriate response considering he was here to rescue her, not to be seduced. Again.

Bathroom time, she thought, seeking an escape. She rolled to the side, groaning at the unexpected pounding in her head.

"Still in pain?" he asked in a gruff voice.

"Only when I move."

"Then don't," he suggested, laughter in his tone.

She closed her eyes tighter and said, "I need the bathroom."

He was up in an instant, coming around her side of the bed. "Let's go. I'll help you."

She managed not to shake her head, catching herself in time. "I'm okay. I just need to brace myself for the movement."

He waited for her to push into a sitting position before bending down and wrapping an arm around her, pulling her slowly to standing. Between his lifting and her shifting, her tank top pulled down beneath one breast, exposing her to the cool air. And she'd been in such a rush to leave the hospital, she hadn't put her bra back on.

"Shit." Tyler quickly yanked her top back in place, but her cheeks burned with embarrassment.

"I can go myself. Please," she said in a small voice.

"Call me if you need me. Don't be a martyr."

At least he'd left her with a tiny bit of dignity, she thought, and she made her way across the room. She took care of business and washed up, splashing cold water on her cheeks and cleaning herself up as best she could. She was surprised to find a travel-sized toothpaste on the counter along with a small deodorant and figured he'd called down to the front desk and asked for whatever toiletries they had on hand. She used those too, then ran her fingers through her tangled hair.

One look in the mirror told her she was a mess, but Tyler had already seen . . . well, everything. It wasn't like she was going to impress him. He was here to do his sister a favor and rescue her best friend. Nothing more.

She groaned and headed back out to face him.

"So I called downstairs while you were sleeping, and apparently the chef took off for the night. Everyone's in a panic, trying to make sure their families are safe. I had them bring up what they could. We have fruit, crackers, chips, and cookies. The best the hotel has to offer," he said wryly

She hadn't thought she'd be hungry, but her stomach grumbled loudly, and he grinned.

"Take your pick." He pointed to the table of food.

Outside, through the one window in the room, the wind whistled through the trees. It was dark and impossible to see what was going on there. "Is it bad?" she asked.

He shrugged. "I'm hoping it'll blow over by morning. The pilot can get us out of here once the winds die down and the runway is clear."

She nodded and settled into a chair at the table. "Thank you again for coming."

He waved off her comment, as if his appearance on the island meant nothing. "You're family."

"You're a liar." She looked up at him and caught the flush highlighting his cheekbones.

"You're right," he admitted.

She winced but knew she deserved that comment. She'd stopped being family the night she'd sneaked into his room.

Forcing herself to do it, she met his gaze. "I'm sorry. I climbed into your bed and that was stupid. Wrong." Of course, she'd been in love with him for years and had spent the evening prior to that drinking schnapps with his sister. She'd been tipsy and had gotten her bravery from alcohol. All idiotic and childish.

"I appreciate that, but I didn't handle things much better."

She forced a smile. "Maybe not, but when the sex sucks, can't really blame a guy for saying so." Of course, she'd been in heaven up until that point.

True, he'd tried to push her away, but she'd plastered herself against him, her flimsy shirt no barrier against his warm, hard chest. And he'd smelled so good she'd buried her face against his cheek for a minute before kissing him . . . and he'd kissed her back. Especially once her sex slid over his boxer briefs. There'd been no going back then.

And Ella, in her tipsy state, with her silly, girlish dreams, had thought it'd meant something to him. That she'd meant something. Sure, it'd hurt at first, and he'd been shocked when he'd discovered that barrier, but soon he'd been thrusting into her and she hadn't cared about the discomfort. It was Tyler. Tyler, whom she'd secretly longed for for years. It was a dream come true.

Until it wasn't.

"Tell me you're on fucking birth control," Tyler had said, his handsome face contorted with anger.

She'd managed a nod, her hair hanging over her shoulder, and she was grateful for it, hoping maybe if she looked away, he wouldn't see her tears. She'd been on the pill for period problems. She hadn't been that stupid. Well, she had been. He hadn't used a condom. God, what had she been thinking, crawling into his bed uninvited?

Sure, he'd had his own wing of the house, but still . . . his mother was on the other side, and so were his sisters. Horrific embarrassment flooded her.

"It's okay," she'd said, not wanting him to be mad at her. She'd been upset enough with herself.

She'd reached out and touched his bare chest, his skin hot to her fingertips. And she'd wanted to kiss him again, to go back to where they'd been when this had started.

Before she could try, his lips had curled downward in disgust. "No, it isn't okay. It was a big fucking mistake. A mess, and you better believe it won't be happening again."

Horrified, she'd scrambled off him with tears falling down her cheeks as she'd grabbed her clothes, pulled on her long shirt, shaking and trying not to lose it in front of him. Finally, she'd gotten herself together and had run, slamming the door behind her.

She'd silently cried herself to sleep next to an already passed-out Avery. And when she'd woken up in the morning, Tyler had been gone. His mother had said he'd been called back to base, but Ella had known better. He couldn't wait to get away from her and put that horrible sexual experience behind him. And she couldn't blame him.

But she could blame him for how he'd handled it. On that, they agreed. Because Tyler Darc had been her first. He'd broken her heart and set the stage for every guy who came after him.

After Tyler, Ella had chosen men very carefully—and they weren't handsome, sexy men from wealthy families with big egos and high expectations. She didn't come from Tyler's world and knew better than to think she was good enough to keep him or anyone like him. She kept her distance from the men she met through work, men with money and swagger, who asked her out. She didn't want a guy who'd assume she was sexually experienced . . . only to be disappointed in the end.

Like Tyler had been.

"Hey."

She shook herself out of the past and realized he'd knelt down beside her.

"What do you mean, when the sex sucks?" he asked in what sounded like disbelief. He looked up at her, his dark hair falling over his forehead, his navy-blue eyes with hints of violet staring at her intently.

They were really going to discuss this? Hadn't she been through enough today? She blew out a long breath. "I saw the look on your face after, Tyler. Not to mention you called me a mistake. A mess. You couldn't push me away from you fast enough. Believe me, I got the message."

"Apparently you got the wrong one. I was pissed at myself. I was more of an adult than you were. Drunk or not, I knew better."

She narrowed her gaze, unsure of whether or not to believe him. "I appreciate you saying that. Trying to make things right. Us being more civil will help when we're with Avery and your family. It'll be easier than trying to avoid each other."

He blinked at her. "Ella, that's not all I'm doing. I'm telling you the truth. I fucked up and I'm sorry."

"Thanks. I'm glad we can move forward as friends." They'd each apologized.

She could live with that. It was better than what she'd had before.

Tyler couldn't believe his ears. He'd finally set the record straight, and she didn't believe him. *Because you screwed her over after her first time.* He'd hurt her, and somewhere deep down, she still hadn't gotten over it. He'd seen it in her expression, and it broke his heart.

He watched in silence as she popped a grape into her mouth and chewed, followed by cheese and crackers. His gaze settled on her lips, full and puckered as she ate, and of course, all he could think about was those lips surrounding his cock.

He shook his head to clear his thoughts before they could travel any further. "I think we should talk about the mugging," he said, changing the subject. "Any idea what people could be looking for?" he asked, hoping she didn't notice his desire-filled voice.

"No. And I don't even know if anything's missing from my old room."

"As soon as the police do their job there, we can go back in and you can check. I called the front desk, and someone should be by to take a look and talk to you."

She shrugged. "They talked to me in the hospital. I don't know any more now than I did then."

He frowned, not liking being in the dark when someone was obviously looking for something and didn't mind hurting her to find it.

"I need a shower," she said, wiping her hands on a napkin and rising to her feet.

"I'm not sure that's a good idea. You may not be steady. What if you get dizzy?" He stood and walked over to her, ready to help if needed.

"Umm, what are you doing?" She peered up at him, wrinkling her nose in confusion. "It's not like you can join me."

But damn, he wanted to. He cleared his throat. "I can stand outside in case you fall."

"I promise to call you if I need you."

He closed his eyes and prayed for strength. "Fine. Don't make the water too hot and steamy, and don't take too long or I'm coming in to check on you."

She perched her hands on her hips and glared. "Bossy much?"

He clenched his jaw. "You have no idea. Now go. Shower and get back into bed. I'll call downstairs and see what's going on with the storm."

He headed to the hotel phone and picked it up, only to find there was no connection. Great. Using his cell, he called Scott and got as good an update as he could from his brother, who confirmed the storm was still predicted to blow over by morning.

"You okay?" Scott asked him.

"Fucking swell," he muttered.

"Is Ella worse than you thought?"

The shower water turned on, and a vision of her naked beneath the warm stream of water nearly knocked him on his ass. Warm rivulets running over her pale skin, dusky nipples.

Fuck.

He gritted his teeth and answered his brother. "Ella's fine. A bad concussion, but she'll be okay." He, on the other hand, might not survive the night. "How's Meg?" His brother's wife was pregnant and due any minute.

"Uncomfortable and ready. So am I, man."

Tyler grinned at his brother's excitement. Even if he didn't quite get it. Tyler had never been the guy who saw marriage and kids in his future. His past proved he wasn't much good at dealing with emotional upheaval, and what was being married or in a relationship? One big morass of emotions. And when things got tough emotionally, Tyler ran. But as his siblings paired off, one by one, and even his mother was now engaged to a good guy, Tyler found himself . . . lonely. Or should he say *alone*?

"Give Meg my love, and I'll call you when I get home."

"Sure thing. And Ty?" Scott asked before he could disconnect the call.

"Yeah?"

"Tread lightly with Ella. Avery will have your balls if you get involved with her and hurt her."

Tyler stiffened. "Seriously? What makes you think I'd go there?" he said, wincing at the lie. "She's like my little sister." Another lie.

His brother let out a know-it-all laugh. "I see how you look at her when you don't think anyone's noticing."

Fuck. Again.

"I also see how she looks at you. And you bicker like an old married couple, so heed my words. If you aren't serious, don't go there."

"Connection sucks," Tyler said, his third lie in as many minutes. "Talk to you when I'm back in the States."

He hung up on his sibling just as the bathroom door opened and Ella stepped into the room, wrapped in a short white towel and nothing else. Her legs were tanned and longer than he remembered, and he was suddenly assaulted by visions of those limbs wrapped around his waist as he pushed into her wet heat.

Tyler broke into a sweat. "Don't you have clothes?" he barked out.

"Would I be dressed in this if I did? My clothes are grimy from the hospital. Do you have a T-shirt or something I can borrow?" Her cheeks were flushed a pretty pink, and she had a death grip on the top of the towel, looking more vulnerable than sexy, and he cursed under his breath.

Once again, he was being an ass. "Let me look in my duffle." He searched through his bag, using the time to get himself under control before turning to her with a T-shirt in hand.

"Here." He hoped the shirt was long enough so he'd stop thinking about what was underneath . . . especially since he didn't know if she was wearing underwear.

"Thanks." She yanked it from his hands and hurried back into the bathroom.

He ran a hand through his hair and prayed for the strength to survive the night. She returned, her damp hair falling around her face.

"Do you think you're up to talking about the mugging?" he asked. "Maybe I can put some pieces together you haven't thought of that might give us a clue to what someone's looking for."

She nodded. "But honestly, I've been racking my brain, and I can't come up with a thing. I was shopping for gifts for Avery and the girls at the hospital where I volunteer. I walked out with the bag, and the next thing I knew, someone was trying to grab my purse."

"And before that, nobody was following you or bothering you?"

She wrinkled her nose and thought about it before answering. "No."

"Anything valuable in your room?" he asked.

"Again, no. I have some pieces of jewelry in the hotel safe because they were from the shoot, and some of the things I loved and didn't want to leave in the room."

He nodded. "Okay. We'll grab those before we go. In the morning, I want you to look through the room and see if anything is missing." He hadn't wanted to put her through the stress until she was feeling better. And by the morning, any courtesy he was giving the island cops was over.

"Sounds like a plan." She pulled self-consciously at the hem of his shirt. "Umm, Tyler?"

"Yeah?" he asked, his voice gruff.

"Thank you. Really. I appreciate you coming down here to help me."

They stared at each other for a long while, the tension an uncomfortable mix of awkwardness, neither one of them knowing what to say or do, and distinct sexual awareness thrumming through the air.

"I'm going to turn in. My head hurts and I'm exhausted," she finally said, breaking eye contact.

"I'll be there shortly." He didn't want to think about the rest of the night sharing the bed with a woman he wanted . . . but couldn't, shouldn't have.

Ella woke up feeling more rested and in less pain. She breathed in deep and was surrounded by a distinctly musky scent that sent tingles of awareness shooting through her veins.

"Tyler," she murmured, belatedly realizing she'd spoken out loud.

"Right here."

And he was. Although she'd started out on the very far side of the king-size bed, she'd rolled toward the center in the middle of the night. She opened her eyes and found herself looking into his navy-blue eyes.

"Hey," she said, embarrassed.

"Hey yourself." His voice sounded gruffer in the morning. And she liked it.

"How do you feel?" he asked.

"Better."

"Good. That's good."

She nodded, incredibly aware of his big body so close to hers, the warmth of his skin, and the full lips just begging to be kissed. All she had to do was lean a centimeter closer and her mouth would be on his. He wasn't shifting away, just staring at her with those sexy eyes.

She moaned, the soft sound escaping without intent. Then she couldn't say who moved first, only that finally, blessedly, his mouth took possession of hers. His lips were firm as he pushed inside and devoured her like he'd been starving and just given a feast. She kissed him back just as eagerly, savoring every stroke of his masterful tongue. He was masculine and in control, able to awaken her senses with just a kiss, and her body responded. Her back arched, her breasts brushed against his bare chest, and her already tight nipples puckered into harder peaks.

His strong hands came to rest on her waist, and as his fingers splayed over her stomach, he maneuvered her closer, his hot, hard erection cushioned in the heat of her sex. Waves of unexpected desire shot through her, and she gripped his hair in her hands, kissing him harder, her hips circling back and forth over his straining shaft. Only her barely there panties kept her from the insanity of his cock thrusting into her willing body.

Warning bells went off in her head, but she was too far gone to heed them. Until his fingers slid up her sides, gliding over her skin, reaching beneath her shirt, and coming to rest beneath her breasts.

She wanted to ignore the continued worry creeping in behind the arousal, but when his fingers glided over her nipples, she jerked back, memories of his reaction after he'd pushed her away much stronger than the sensual feelings he aroused in the present. She'd been so lost in being with him then that not even the pain of her first time had mattered until the sharp snap of his angry tone had burst her fantasy.

She hadn't been enough for him then, no matter what he claimed today, and no way could she be enough for him now. She was, and always would be, a girl who was good enough to be used—by her father for bone marrow to save her step-mother and by Tyler for sex and nothing after. Both men had defined her expectations. Nobody would protect her. Nobody would look after her except herself.

"I . . . can't. This isn't a good idea."

He stared at her for a silent while, until finally he spoke. "I respect what you're saying. I even agree. But—and let me be crystal clear this time—not for the reasons you're think-ing. I want you, Ella. I've always wanted you."

She blinked in surprise.

Yesterday he'd explained that his anger hadn't been at her, it had been at himself. But that didn't change her insecuri-ties or the fact that during all her sexual encounters since, she'd had Tyler's disgust ringing in her brain. She could never make herself enjoy the physical act because the one man she'd wanted had rejected her so harshly and at such a vulnerable age and time.

She ran her tongue over her dry lips. "So you were serious? You weren't just trying to make me feel better?" The sex hadn't sucked for him?

"No, sweet girl, the sex definitely didn't suck."

A full-body shiver took hold, a result of the endearment and heartfelt words.

"And if . . . or when it happens again," he continued, "it definitely won't suck then either."

Her eyes opened so wide she imagined they were saucers in her face. "Okay then." She scrambled for the far side of the bed and rose to her feet. Shaking, she said, "I need to get dressed."

An amused grin pulled at his lips, and she glanced away, unable to face what he was insinuating.

At least not yet.

"I'll check on the weather and flight plan. Then we can get the hotel to let you back into your room so you can pack up your things. I don't give a shit if the cops are too busy to check things out. We're going home."

She nodded, all too happy to get out of there. Back to real life, where she didn't have to deal with Tyler Dare, his tousled hair, sexy bedroom eyes, and hot kisses.

## Chapter Three

With his blood still running hot in his veins, Tyler accompanied Ella to her trashed hotel room. It hurt him to see the pained look in her eyes when she took in how carelessly her clothing and possessions had been tossed around. But to her credit, she straightened her shoulders and forged ahead.

What had he been thinking, insinuating he could sleep with her again? She deserved so much more than a guy whose past consisted of fucking up when things got tough.

Memories of Jack, his best friend in the army, resurfaced, and with Ella busy, he couldn't hold them back. Tyler appreciated his time in the army for what it was, for teaching him to become tougher, stronger, the man his father had told him to be. But he'd hated every minute of the reality. The gritty sand in the Middle East, the ridiculously hot temperatures while they carried too many pounds of clothing and equipment on their sweating bodies. And death. Everywhere. Men, women, children. The sound of gunfire, bombs, IEDs . . .

Jack hadn't been able to handle the thought of those. He'd wanted out and said so over and over again. But hell, they'd all wanted out. Tyler, too, couldn't wait till their tour was over. With six months and counting, he'd known he could pull through. His mistake had been in thinking Jack could too. His friend had gone AWOL and fucking gotten himself killed, leaving a wife and a baby at home. And once again, Tyler was left feeling like if he'd only said something, he might have saved his friend.

The same way he could have warned his mother. And the same way he could have spared Ella the humiliation and pain she'd clearly suffered all these years if only he'd stuck around afterward and faced her like a man.

Jack's death had put a mirror to Tyler's flaws. It'd brought him home knowing he had to do better but uncertain if he had it in him. So he had no business getting involved with Ella physically when emotionally he could still decimate her.

Realizing he'd been lost in thought, he glanced over only to find she, too, was lost in the devastation of her room. He took in the mess. Her suitcase was already open and had obviously been searched. With trembling hands, she threw her clothes into the luggage, taking time to examine each piece as if she could find answers. Unable to stand it a second longer, he stepped up behind her and grasped her shoulders, turning her to face him.

He wasn't surprised to see tears in her eyes. "It's just stuff. Things that can be replaced."

She nodded. "I know, but I feel so violated." She sniffed and glanced around the room. "Someone touched my things." She stared at the T-shirt in her hand and dropped it as if it were contaminated.

In his line of business, Tyler had seen similar reactions before. It was worse when someone's home had been broken into, leaving them forced to come to terms with the fact that their sanctuary, a place they returned to day in and day out, would never feel safe again.

He pushed the suitcase away. "Leave everything that doesn't have special meaning. You can replace it at home."

She blinked up at him. "But it's expensive."

He shrugged, aware she wasn't the type of woman to waste money, that she hadn't come from a world of privilege. He knew he was being extreme, but he'd seen her strength, and he knew what she'd do.

"Will you wear any of this again knowing someone touched it? If so, I'm more than happy to pack it up for you. But if you're that upset, take what you want, and then we'll grab your stuff from the hotel safe and get the hell out of Dodge."

She straightened her shoulders and began to toss everything into the suitcase with more determination than before. "No way am I going to let some asshole beat me down," she muttered, adding the last item of clothing she could find from the floor.

Reverse psychology worked every time. But he admired her strength and couldn't help but grin at her renewed spirit. That was the young girl he'd met, surviving needles and tests and more at the hospital while her father hovered over her ill stepmother, not his petite daughter.

Tyler was glad to see that spunk still lived inside her. He found it easier to focus on this side of Ella than the vulnerable woman who'd pulled away from him in bed. He hated knowing that he'd hurt her, and even more, that the pain had stuck with her all these years. There was a lot he didn't know about Ella and the woman she'd become. Any time his sister spoke of her, Tyler tuned her out, not wanting to deal with the lie between him and Avery or the self-loathing he always experienced because of how he'd behaved afterward.

But now, he had an opening. Apology given, he could try, at least, to put his own guilt aside and deal with Ella as a woman. A woman he still had extremely hot chemistry with. A woman he both liked and admired. And a woman he wanted to get to know better. Shit.

Pushing those thoughts aside to deal with back home, he refocused on getting them out of there. While Ella retrieved her toiletries from the bathroom and packed them too, Tyler checked the drawers and closet, although all were open and nothing was left inside.

A little while later, she'd emptied the hotel safe and packed its contents up, adding them to her bags. She slid one particular piece, a long blue necklace, over her head and patted it against her chest. "Now I'm ready," she said, her hazel eyes alight with excitement. She was as ready to blow this joint as he was.

"We just need to check out."

They stopped at the front desk, where an older woman sat behind the counter. "All set?" she asked.

Ella nodded, placing a pair of sunglasses on top of her head.

"There's no charge to either of you for last night's room. Between the storm and the robbery, we're just so sorry you had an unpleasant stay on our island."

"We appreciate that," Tyler said. Considering they hadn't had a solid meal, he was glad he didn't have to argue about paying.

"I need to close out my account for the earlier part of my trip," Ella said.

"Our computers aren't working today. I'm going to have to mail you the bill," she said regretfully. "It'll go on the credit card you left when you checked in. Any issues, just give us a call."

"I will."

"Do you need a ride to the airport?" the clerk asked.

"We do," he said, all too eager to leave.

The clerk gestured to a man sitting by a desk near the door. "Matteo can help you."

"I'll be right back," Tyler said, heading over to arrange their transportation and returning almost immediately. "He said a cab would be here any minute."

"Okay, I'm ready." Ella reached for her luggage, but he beat her to it, grabbing the handle.

"Before you go, I just want to say that I love your necklace," the woman behind the desk said.

Ella lifted the blue amulet trimmed in gold. "Thank you. It was part of the photo shoot. My boss asked me to make sure it got home. I figure my best bet is to wear it."

The desk clerk leaned over the counter, and Ella let her look more closely at the piece while Tyler tapped his foot with impatience. Though he had sisters and should be used to discussions about jewelry and makeup, it was because he'd grown up with two females that he lacked a healthy tolerance for it.

"You know, it looks like a replica of an item stolen from a museum on the island years ago."

He perked up at the word *stolen*. Part of the job, he supposed.

"Legend has it that one of the earlier kings had it designed for his cousin's bride. It was part of a collection in the national museum until it was stolen. There have been replicas floating around for years."

"I didn't know it had such history attached to it. That's fascinating," Ella murmured, eyes twinkling as she studied the necklace. "I'll have to look into it some more when I get home."

The woman smiled. "You should do that. It's interesting. Anyway, Matteo's gesturing for you. Your cab's here. Have a safe trip back."

"Thank you," he and Ella said at the same time.

They stowed the bags and climbed into the cab, and the driver, a chatty man, explained that St. Lucia had escaped the worst of the hurricane, experiencing some power outages and minimal damage.

They just weren't equipped for heavy outages, and the hotel, a place with only thirty-eight rooms, had lost phone service. And the help had left to head to their homes, Tyler thought, his stomach growling.

"Hungry?" Ella asked with a grin.

"Starving. I hope Ian has the plane well stocked because I could eat a horse," he muttered.

"Ahh, to be rich and famous," she said with a laugh.

"Rich. Thank God I'm not the famous one in the family." He shuddered at the thought. "My father brought enough notoriety on us as kids to last a lifetime." A mistress, a second family . . . the kids at school had had a field day bullying the Dares. Until Ian, Scott, and Tyler had stood up for themselves and their sisters. Nobody had bothered the Dares ever again.

"I'm sorry. That was a tactless joke."

"You don't have to censor your words around me. It is what it is. Or was. We've all come to terms with it."

"Have you?" she asked, staring too perceptively into his eyes, with understanding that made him want to confide in her.

He'd just run through all his faults hours earlier. He had no desire to do it again. "Not really," he heard himself saying, admitting it because she'd asked and he wanted her to know. "But it's too long to discuss on a short cab ride."

"If you ever want to talk about it, I'm here." And with that, she respected his wishes and closed her eyes, shutting out him and the world.

Ella leaned her head back, resting, but he could tell from the strain around her mouth she was in more pain than she let on. Unable to help himself, he slid his hand over hers, meaning to comfort. The spark of desire he felt on touching her was undeniable, and his cock jerked in response to the heated feel of her soft skin.

Her lashes fluttered open, and she turned her head, meeting his gaze, the flow of awareness between them strong.

"We're here," the cab driver said, breaking the sensual spell.

Tyler glanced out the window as they pulled into the large area of the airport where private planes were stowed.

Another cab pulled up close behind them. Too close, and hit the cab's back bumper. Their taxi driver let out a string of curses. "He's been following too close ever since we left the hotel, the bastard."

Tyler narrowed his gaze. He wasn't one for coincidences, and between Ella's mugging, her hotel room break-in, and now this, he wanted to get her off the island immediately. Even if this incident had nothing to do with her, and it probably didn't, his senses were tingling and everything felt off. He'd be happier when they were back in the US and this island and her nightmare were behind them.

The driver hopped out of the car and confronted the other driver.

"Wait here," Tyler said. He exited the vehicle and looked around, assuring himself that it seemed to be just an accident before returning to help Ella out of the car.

"We need our bags," he said to the driver, interrupting his angry tirade. The bumper tap was just that, no damage, and it was easy to pop the trunk and get their luggage. Tyler paid, tipped the man, and left him to his issues.

They entered a small building, where they checked in and were surrounded by more people than Tyler had expected. He clasped Ella's hand and held on tight, keeping her by his side, all the while his gut twisting uncomfortably.

"Tyler?"

"It's fine. Just stick close," he said, unwilling to explain the unexplainable.

Finally, they headed out onto the tarmac, where a man in a golf cart drove them to Ian's fueled and waiting plane. They boarded and headed home, but Tyler remained uneasy.

The private jet was a luxury unknown to Ella. From the discreet flight attendant catering to their every need to the plush seats and room to walk around, she was overwhelmed and out of her element. Add the concussion and the events of the last forty-eight hours, and no sooner had she settled into the comfy chair and buckled in than she tipped her head back and fell asleep.

She woke up to find Tyler studying her intently.

"I hope I wasn't snoring," she said, uncomfortably aware of how alone they were in the cabin. How alone they'd been in the hotel room, and what had almost happened between them. What she still wanted to happen, despite knowing better.

He grinned. "That's my secret to keep."

She blushed, feeling the heat rush to her face.

"We're landing soon," he said. "I left my SUV at the airport, so I'll drive you home."

She glanced out the window at the clear blue skies and the ocean below. Soon enough, she'd be seeing the shoreline of Miami. Of home. Reality. "I think I've put you out enough. I can take a cab."

"Ella." He placed a hand on her bare knee, below the hem of her skirt, his warm touch a brand on her flesh. "I said I'd take you home," he said in that commanding voice so common to the Dare men.

And when Tyler used that tone, everything inside Ella stilled, compelled to listen. She shivered at his touch, but her mind wasn't on her physical reaction but the emotional one.

She wasn't used to anyone looking out for her in any way.

She'd had a family once, and then her mom had died of a stroke when Ella was five. After that, it was just Ella and her dad, until he'd met and married Janice Freeman when Ella was eight. At first she'd been excited to have another woman in the house. She'd missed her mom and having someone to talk to, shop with, and do things with like her friends did with their moms. But Janice was a cold woman with no interest in having a daughter. She'd had her twelve-year-old son, Drew, and didn't need another child. To this day, Ella wasn't sure why the two had married, but she marked it as the day her relationship with her father had ended.

Harry Shaw had doted on his new wife, spent time making his stepson happy, and when Janice was diagnosed with cancer, he'd done as he'd been doing for the last two years: put his wife's needs before his only daughter's. After visiting her comatose mother in the hospital, Ella was petrified of hospitals and anything doctor-related, especially needles. Even so, he hadn't looked far for the bone marrow donor, zeroing in on a frightened, lonely little girl to do the right thing when Janice's son wasn't a match.

The irony was that Janice hadn't appreciated the sacrifice. Having received a second chance, after she'd recovered, she'd dumped Harry Shaw for a younger, wealthier man in her zeal to really live.

Had Harry stepped up and become Ella's parent then? No, he'd chosen to give his affection to alcohol instead. Nothing had been able to stop his downward spiral, not even a thirteen-year-old child who needed him. And a year later, after a devastating car crash, he was found guilty of DUI vehicular homicide, and was now serving time in prison. The aunt Ella had gone to live with was a widow with no children, who mostly left Ella alone. Was it any wonder her vacations with Avery and the Dare family had been a fairy tale and a dream come true for Ella?

But given her life, was she used to anyone worrying if she went home by herself? Taking care of her when she was sick? No, she was not. She didn't know what to make of the fact that Tyler wanted to be there for her now.

But from the determined look in his eyes and the set of his jaw, he wouldn't take no for an answer.

So she went from the private jet to the luxury passenger seat of his black Range Rover. The truck smelled like Tyler, his musky masculine scent and distinctive cologne something she'd recognize in the dark, or blindfolded. He made a few calls while they drove, catching up with his business, and she watched the palm trees go by as they headed for her apartment.

At this point, she didn't know if her life was a dizzying blur because of the concussion or Tyler Dare's persistent presence.

He parked in a visitor's spot and headed inside. As he rolled her suitcase down the hall, he turned to her. "You never got a roommate after Avery moved in with Grey?"

She shook her head. "I'm looking, but I'm picky. I'm fortunate that my boss is generous, but I'm going to have to pull the trigger soon or move." She was about to dig into her purse for her keys when she remembered. "My keys were in my purse, which was stolen." She slumped against the wall, frustration overtaking her.

"Good thing I'm ahead of you," he said, knocking on her door. "Avery had the locks changed today. She has a set of keys for you inside."

"You're back!" Avery flung the door open and threw herself at Ella, pulling her into the tightest hug she'd ever experienced.

To her mortification, tears filled her eyes, and she broke down for the first time since the mugging and waking up all alone in the hospital in St. Lucia.

Tyler never knew what to do when a woman cried, and given he'd been raised with two sisters, he had plenty of experience.

Though he should be used to it, he found himself emotionally wrecked by Ella's tears, affected by her pain, both of which told him there was more to him wanting to be with her than a sexual fling. Again, none of which he could allow to matter.

He studied his sister, her dark hair highlighted with blonde, wearing a strappy dress and flat sandals, in stark contrast with Ella, her light brown hair shorter than Avery's, her outfit more casual. He couldn't tear his gaze from Ella's trembling form. Even as he wondered what the hell it was about her that had always gotten past his barriers, he already knew. He had a pattern of behavior that could only hurt her if they got emotionally involved.

As he liked to point out to himself, if only so he never forgot it, when things got tough, Tyler ran instead of facing his problems head on. And though he was home now, trying to prove he'd learned from the past, before he told any woman—especially Ella—she could count on him for the long haul, he needed to know he not only meant it but could act on his intentions.

Otherwise he'd be left with one more unresolved issue, one more person he'd screwed with his behavior. No better than his father, no better than Jack Gibson, his fellow soldier and friend who'd gone AWOL and, in doing so, gotten himself killed, leaving Serena and their baby daughter behind.

He glanced at the women as Avery hugged Ella one more time. "Let's go inside."

"Good idea. Is Grey here?" Tyler asked, eager to move along from their emotional reunion and the introspection it inspired.

"He's home getting ready for our trip to LA. He's recording this week, remember?" she asked as they stepped into the apartment and she shut the door behind them.

He parked Ella's rolling bag against the wall, and she headed straight for the sofa in the living room, falling into it with a thud.

"Ouch," she muttered, bracing her head in her hands. "That wasn't a smart move."

He winced. Having had a concussion, he could imagine her pain.

"Can I get you anything?" Avery asked.

"No. I just really appreciate everything you did for me, sending Tyler down and being here now." She reached out and squeezed Avery's hand.

"Do you think I'd leave you stranded?" Avery blinked back tears. "I'm just glad you're okay. Now, I brought a bag, and I can stay tonight and even the night after, but I'm leaving in two days, and we're going to have to make sure you're taken care of." Avery not-so-subtly looked Tyler in the eye.

He coughed, unprepared for what she was insinuating—that he continue to look out for Ella and the fact that Avery would be okay with it.

"No!" Ella pushed herself up on the sofa. "You go home to Grey and pack for your trip. You've been looking forward to traveling with him for this new recording session, and nothing is going to ruin it. I'm a big girl, and I've been taking care of myself for a while now. I'll be fine."

Avery turned on her full-fledged pout. "Well, you know I'm not going to let you fall back into ultraindependent mode. Not when you've been through so much. What if you don't feel well in the middle of the night or you get dizzy? Tyler, tell her I'm right."

"He'll do no such thing," Ella said before Tyler could get a word in between the two bickering women. "The doctor released me from the hospital, so he must have been sure it was safe."

"He released you into Tyler's care. You said yourself they wouldn't let you leave alone."

"The danger period has passed." She shot Tyler a pleading look.

"What if I promise to come by after work tomorrow and check on her?" he heard himself suggesting to his sister. Giving himself the opening he needed to see Ella again.

Avery sighed. "Well, if that's all I'll get out of you two stubborn people, I'll take it. But I'm calling to check on you before bedtime. And as soon as I wake up in the morning."

"Deal," Ella said quickly, obviously before Avery changed her mind and insisted on a full-time babysitter again.

She gave Tyler a grateful look, piercing him with those doe eyes, and he didn't want to leave.

Instead, knowing it was smarter, he straightened, preparing to head out. "Can I get you anything before I go?" he asked.

She shook her head. "You've done so much. More than anyone's done for me before."

This wasn't the first time, on the island and again now, that she'd alluded to the fact that she was used to being on her own. He came from a big family where people stepped up for each other. When he was younger, he'd always had his siblings and his parents around him, his mother as a constant presence, his father as a larger-than-life icon until that idolization had been blown to smithereens.

When Tyler had taken off to be on his own, it was by choice. He couldn't imagine being alone out of necessity, and his gut told him that was what had happened to Ella. He was aware of some vague details about her past: that her mother had died when she was young, her father had remarried, she'd given bone marrow to her stepmom, and her father was now in prison. Beyond that, there was little he knew about her personal life.

Now he wanted to delve deeper, but Tyler promised himself he'd take the time to be very sure of himself, of her . . . of them, before stepping up in a way that'd hurt Ella more than she'd already been hurt.

Sex he knew how to handle, and there was no doubt he meant to sweet-talk his way into her bed. She wanted him as much as he did her. But even if he didn't understand all the reasons why, he knew he needed to be more careful with her heart.

# Chapter Four

Ella was exhausted, and though she wanted nothing more than to take a long, hot shower and crawl into bed, she understood she needed to talk to Avery first. Her friend had gone above and beyond for her; she always had.

"So now that Tyler's gone, want to tell me what's up with you two?" Avery asked as she headed for the kitchen and then poured them both a glass of orange juice.

"Where did that come from? My refrigerator was empty when I left," Ella said, accepting the glass and taking a refreshing sip.

"I know you like to empty it out when you leave, so I stopped by the grocery store on the way here today."

Ella shook her head, the tears she kept trying to hold back returning again. She sniffed and dabbed at her eyes with her free hand. "You're too good to me."

"And that's your problem. You really believe that."

"I have good reason," Ella muttered, but she really didn't want to get into deep conversation. "I love you, I'm grateful, and if I don't get some sleep, I'm going to pass out on you anyway. So would you be insulted if I—"

"Ask me to leave?" Avery asked with a grin. "Of course not. But I mean it when I say I'm going to be checking up on you."

"You're the sister I never had." Ella pulled her friend into a tight hug.

"You're my second sister," Avery said. She eased back and grinned. "Can't get rid of Olivia, as much as I used to want to."

Ella laughed.

"I'm glad things seem more normal between you and Tyler. Usually when you two are together, you're bickering like . . . siblings."

More like sexually attracted adults, but no way was Ella going there. She had no doubt that Tyler had made his promise to check on her just to get Avery off both of their backs. No doubt, come tomorrow, she'd be back to her normal life, and Tyler would have forgotten all about a promise to his sister.

The next day, after an uneasy night's sleep, a combination of jumpiness after her experience on the island and discomfort from the bump on her head, she woke up still tired. She showered, careful not to jostle her head too much since the bruising and swelling were still evident to the touch. But as she'd learned, the best way to deal with life was to push through it. So after Avery checked in as promised and Ella wished her a safe trip to LA, she called her boss, grateful she had a home phone because she'd lost her cell in the mugging.

Angie answered on the first ring. "Darling, I've been so worried about you!" she said, because Ella had called her from St. Lucia, downplaying her situation but letting her know about the mugging and room break-in.

Although Angie had an affectation in her speech, so the word sounded more like *dahling*, the older woman had always been warm and caring toward Ella, and Ella heard the concern in her voice now.

"I'm home and I'm safe," Ella said. "I know you told me to take some time off, but I'm ready to work." To get back to normal. "Are you in the office today? I'd love to see the shots we took on the island."

"I have a meeting in the Keys today, so I won't be in. But you can meet me first thing tomorrow, and I'll bring the pictures in. In the meantime, I insist you see a doctor here. Make sure you're really all right."

"It's just a concussion," Ella promised her. "But since you won't be in today, I promise to rest." She crossed her fingers behind her back, knowing she'd use her day off to run errands. "How's that?"

"Sounds like it's as good as I'm going to get, so I'll take it. So . . . do you have the amulet?"

"Yes. I told you, I kept it in the hotel safe with the other pieces, so it wasn't in the room when it was broken into. Don't worry. I'll bring everything with me tomorrow."

"No!" Angie said, her tone sharp. "I mean, don't worry about it for now," she said, her voice back to normal. "Keep it somewhere safe. When we need everything for another shoot, so you can give it back to me then."

Ella shrugged. "Okay, I'll do that. Have fun in the Keys."

"Yes, wish me luck," she said cryptically.

Ella had no idea what she was referring to. "Good luck," she said, rolling her eyes, knowing her boss could be eccentric as well as temperamental.

"See you tomorrow, dear."

"Bye." Ella disconnected the call, then spent the next hour or more canceling credit cards and calling the bank. She locked the amulet in the safe in the closet of Avery's old room.

Then she headed out, starting at the bank for a new debit card, then heading to the Department of Motor Vehicles to get a new license, followed by a trip to purchase a new cell phone. More than once, she had an uneasy feeling she couldn't shake. She'd think she heard someone, look over her shoulder, but no one was there. Or look in her rearview mirror and think she was being followed. After St. Lucia, she felt paranoid and ridiculous, and she tried to push her unease out of her mind.

With the dreaded chores from the mugging complete, she made her way to the Dollar Store, where she bought colorful beads and necklaces for the kids at the hospital to replace what had been stolen when she was attacked. She caught sight of a dark-haired man staring at her at the store. She glanced at him, and he waved and walked away. Crazy. She was losing her mind.

She refocused on the children, who would be excited to get presents, and it wouldn't matter to them whether or not they came from the Caribbean. She also bought some cupcakes, because who didn't like a special treat? And she needed one herself after the crazy couple of days she'd had. She had a special affinity for these kids, not because she'd ever been sick like them but because she'd spent time in the hospital. Despite her dislike of everything having to do with hospitals, first because of her mother and then thanks to her bone marrow donation, she never wanted another child to feel the fear that she had.

Her father had spent his time at her stepmother's bedside, praying for her to get better. Ella had been alone during and after the donation, more so when she'd gone home afterward and Janice had remained hospitalized. Ella had been left in her stepbrother's care, and while Drew had never abused her, he hadn't paid attention to her either. He'd resented having to look after her when he could be with his friends or at the hospital with his mom. Ella might as well have been alone.

While some of the kids Ella visited today had parents who were there for them twenty-four seven, others were alone while their mom or dad worked during the day. Ella liked to fill in those gaps, and she spent the better part of the afternoon watching TV and telling stories about the Caribbean island and the hurricane she really hadn't experienced and making up tales about the amulet necklace the clerk had told her about, which the kids were fascinated by.

Finally, exhausted and head pounding from overdoing it too soon, she stopped at the supermarket so she could add to the items Avery had purchased for her, including buying sushi for dinner.

She returned to her apartment to find Tyler waiting outside her door, foot tapping, eyeing her with a combination of concern and annoyance.

Tyler had been standing in the hallway for a good half hour waiting for Ella outside her apartment. Her cell had been stolen with her purse so he couldn't call her to ask where the hell she was. Hadn't he told her he'd be checking in after work?

Finally, the elevator doors opened and she walked out, wearing a lavender tank top and a soft white skirt floating around her thighs, casual as you please, grocery bags in hand. He was worked up, torn between worry and frustration.

"What are you doing here?" she asked, seeming genuinely surprised to see him.

Which pissed him off to no end. She hadn't believed he'd be here for her. "We agreed I'd be checking in on you after work today."

"You said you would but—"

"You didn't think it was important for you to be here when I did?" he asked.

She blinked up at him, giving him his first real glimpse of the exhaustion lining her face and the dark circles under her eyes, causing much of the anger to seep out of him. Instead, he wanted to take her in his arms and ease the strain she was obviously under. And when had that ever happened? When had he ever wanted to take care of a woman who wasn't family? She'd gotten under his skin, that much he knew.

"Of course not. I just didn't . . ." She trailed off, and he had no problem filling in the blanks.

"You didn't think I was serious about stopping by," he said, unsure whether to be more hurt or annoyed that for the second time in as many days, she hadn't taken him at his word. Another first—that he cared what she thought of him.

"I'm sorry. It's just that—"

"Don't worry about it." He'd deal with her trust issues later, because it was clear to him she had many. Just as clearly, he intended to be the one to fix them. No, that hadn't been his intention in coming over here. But one look at her and all his priorities had shifted. He hadn't seen her since leaving yesterday, hadn't heard a word. And other than Avery thanking him again for looking after her best friend, his sister hadn't given him any more information about Ella either.

Not knowing how she was—whether she was in pain from the concussion, whether she was scared because she'd been mugged and her room vandalized—left him edgy. He wanted nothing more than to park himself in her apartment and just be there for her, merely cementing what his gut had been telling him from the minute he'd walked into that hospital room and seen her lying there, helpless and vulnerable. He cared. A lot.

He might not be able to commit to anything long term, but he knew he could fix the emotional damage he'd done to her when they'd slept together last, and that suddenly became his goal. But getting past her defenses was going to be more difficult than any op he'd faced while in the army.

He'd have to start slowly and gain her trust, especially after the way he'd shattered it all those years ago. Get her to open up to him. First he had to get her relaxed and settled, because she looked dead on her feet.

"Give me the bags," he said, not waiting but taking the plastic sacks from her hands. "Open the door and let's get this stuff put away."

"Tyler, it's not that I didn't believe you," she said, sadness in her tone.

As crazy as it seemed, he understood. "You didn't have reason to believe me, and I get why, but that's going to stop now. When I say I'm going to do something, I always mean it. And I'm telling you, I'm here to help. You clearly aren't taking good care of yourself and need a keeper. I'm taking on that role."

"Why? Because Avery asked you to?" This time, she sounded pissed off as she fished through her purse for the key to her apartment. "I don't need you to look after me. I'm not some obligation you need to take care of." She shoved the key into the lock and opened the door, letting it slam against the wall. "I can take care of myself. I've—"

"Been doing it for a long time, yeah, I know. I got the message." And he wanted to strangle the parent who'd left her so alone and vulnerable.

His chest hurt at the matter-of-fact way she believed this was how things had to be. He pushed past her and headed inside, hearing the door shut behind him as he put the bags on the counter.

Drawing a deep breath, he turned back to face her. She'd come into the kitchen and leaned against the counter, arms folded across her chest as she studied him, uncertainty in her wide-eyed gaze. Uncertainty he was determined to erase for good. Drawn to her, he stepped closer, until he was in front of her, invading her personal space.

Her eyes widened and her breath hitched at his nearness. His was coming in shallow pants, and the urge to kiss her, to taste her, was almost overwhelming.

He knew he was moving too fast—for her, for him—but he couldn't stop himself or the words that came next. "Maybe you have been on your own for a long time, but you don't have to be anymore. Not if you open yourself up and trust me."

She narrowed her gaze, her soft lips lifting in disbelief. "Trust you. Because you rescued me after your sister asked?"

God, she was stubborn. And that defiance turned him on even more than he cared to admit. "That's not why."

"Really?" she pushed, clearly trying to keep those emotional and physical walls erected between them. "Look, I'm not ungrateful, but so far everything you've done for me has been because Avery begged you to help me."

"Yes, it seems that way—" But he was here because he wanted to be. And from the way his heart pounded hard in his chest, he needed to be.

"Well, I'm not some charity case and—"

He shut her up with a kiss. A hard, long, tongue-dueling, dick-hardening kiss. She braced her hands on his shoulders, and he prepared himself to be pushed away, but instead, she curled her fingers into his skin and gave in, her lips and body softening beneath his onslaught.

He didn't let up, sliding his lips back and forth over hers, his tongue learning all the deep secrets of her mouth. He didn't want to leave her with a single doubt that he was here for her, and only her, because he wanted to be, not because she was some obligation he had to fulfill. Because not only did he want her, he also needed to show her how different things could be between them. Replace the bad memories with good ones, so when they inevitably parted this time, she wouldn't doubt herself, how desirable she was, or her ability to please a man. Not that he wanted to think about other men when she was in his arms.

At the thought, he grew more possessive, angling his head for a deeper kiss. She slid her hands up his shoulders to his head, her fingers tangling in his hair, her lips warm and supple beneath his. He hoped like hell she was getting the message, because his cock was throbbing and his heart pounding hard in his chest.

He tipped his head, coming up for air for a brief second before diving back in for another kiss that lasted until she hit her head against the cabinets above her head.

"Dammit." She sucked in a breath, and he jerked back, catching the tears filling her eyes from pain.

"Sorry, sweet girl." He reached up and cupped the back of her head in his hand, gently massaging the area around the bump. "You okay?"

She slid a tongue over her now puffy lips and nodded, those hazel eyes wide and hazy with desire as she studied him.

"Did that feel like you're some charity case to me?" he asked, stroking her cheek with his knuckles. "Like I didn't want you with a desperation?"

"No."

Her eyes were glassy, but her expression had softened, and he liked the dreamy look on her face, knowing he'd put it there.

"I don't understand what's happening between us," she murmured.

Join the club, he thought. All he knew was that in the twenty-four hours they'd been apart, he couldn't stop thinking about her, wondering how she was doing, if she was thinking about him too. Quite a change from the guy who'd had to have his arm twisted to face her and their shared past.

"How about you quit overthinking things and just . . . be?" And he'd do the same.

She hesitated, then finally nodded. "I'll try."

He'd take it, he thought and grinned. "Good. Now what's for dinner?"

She smiled, seemingly taking his advice to just let things between them happen naturally.

"Sushi from the market, but I only brought enough for me."

He shrugged, unconcerned. "That's what delivery is for."

Satisfied he'd broken through her walls, at least for now, he turned his attention to food. He ordered in Chinese in addition to the sushi and instead of eating in the kitchen, they settled in around the low table in the living room.

"So what did you do today?" he asked, pushing the last container of moo shu pork aside.

"Made all the calls to replace my stolen credit cards, hit up motor vehicles, replaced my cell—"

"Thank God," he muttered. "At least now I can reach you."

She smiled shyly, and he liked knowing he had the power to affect her emotionally as well as physically.

"Then I went by the hospital to see the kids. I felt bad my gifts were stolen, so I picked up beads and other things at the Dollar Store instead."

"You're amazing with those kids," he said, unable to hide his admiration.

When Avery had been in the hospital donating her bone marrow, seeing all those sick people had made Tyler uncomfortable. He'd never thought about it after that except when he'd finally gotten to know Sienna, his half sister who'd been the recipient. Only then had he realized how lucky they all were she'd survived. But he hadn't been driven to volunteer or give back the way Avery and Ella did. For someone who wasn't given much in the way of love or emotion, Ella gave back selflessly, making him want to show her what it was like to be on the other side. He wanted to give to her and plug the doubts that always seemed to plague her.

She shrugged. "They make it easy. They just want to be loved and get healthy." She rose to her feet and began collecting the dishes.

"I've got that. Why don't you relax while I finish up? You've had a long day."

"I can help. It's just a bump on the head, and I'm getting better," she insisted.

He stood, pleased he towered over her so he could make his point with an advantage. "Sit. Rest. And let me do this for you. My mother didn't raise any slackers." He winked at her as he spoke.

And at the mention of his mom, an amused grin lifted her lips. "True enough. You know, she's the closest thing to a mom I've got," she said, lowering herself back onto the floor and curling her legs beneath her.

His heart squeezed at the admission. "I know your mom passed away when you were little," he said.

"Yeah. She died of a stroke when I was five," she said softly.

He continued to clean up, carrying boxes to the garbage in the kitchen and taking the plates to the sink, all the while hoping she'd continue to open up. "And your father remarried, because that's how you met Avery at the hospital."

"He did, but Janice wasn't all that interested in being my mother."

Considering how quickly and easily the Dares had pulled Ella into their family, especially his mother, Tyler couldn't understand how a woman could marry a guy with a kid and not care for her. "That sucks," he said, unable to come up with something more insightful.

She laughed, the sound lifting the mood caused by the subject matter. "It did suck. But I was young and I did what I had to do, donating bone marrow, because when your father begs, what else can you do? Besides, even if I'd been an adult, could I really have said no?"

He glanced over from the kitchen and caught her lifting her shoulder in a small shrug. "I don't know. There are definitely people who would have said no for lesser reasons than the fact that the woman didn't treat you well."

"Like being scared of hospitals and needles? Or only being ten? Yeah, none of that mattered."

He strode back into the other room, joining her on the sofa and edging in close. He picked up her hand and held it tight. "You know it didn't matter to my father either when he had all his kids tested for Sienna or when the youngest came up the match."

A smile edged her lips. "Why do you think Avery and I bonded so fast and so well? We had a lot in common." She paused in thought before continuing. "And we had a lot of differences too."

"Like what?" he asked.

"Like, I came from a two-bedroom apartment and Avery . . . didn't."

Knowing she was involved in her story and not paying attention, he lifted his free hand and curled a strand of her hair around his finger, feeling the silken strands with his thumb while watching her expressions as she spoke.

"Why does the money make such a difference to you?"

"Asks the person who never had to worry," she said in a teasing tone. "It's not that money differences matter. It's that I saw a whole different world, and it made me aspire to have more."

That much he understood. "Nothing wrong with wanting more. Besides, you achieved your goals, and that's an amazing thing."

She blushed at his obvious appreciation. "Avery's life exposed me to so many more ideas than I ever would have had for a career." She wrapped her hands around her knees and met his gaze. "I'll be forever grateful."

"Well, your friendship did a lot for her when she was suffering from anxiety, so I'd say you're even."

Avery's anxiety issues had alienated her from friends and sometimes even from family, not that the Dares allowed her

to pull away. Having Ella, someone who'd shared such a trau-
matic experience, had definitely helped her through.

"If you say so," Ella said.

"Why do you do that?" he asked, jumping on her
self-deprecation.

"Do what?" She bit into her lower lip and met his gaze.

He shouldn't ask such a harsh question, but he couldn't
hold back either. Not if he wanted to get to know what made
Ella tick. And he did. "Why don't you believe in yourself and
what you bring to the table?"

She studied him intently, her gaze so serious he thought
she could see beneath his skin, and a sense of unease rose
to the surface. He had a feeling he wasn't going to like her
answer—should she choose to share it—and he waited in
silence.

"I didn't realize I do that," she finally admitted. "It must
just slip out."

"Fair enough. But that doesn't change the fact that you feel
it." And he wanted to know why.

She let out a sigh. "How old were you when you found out
about your father's other kids?"

He stiffened as he always did when having this discussion,
but he might as well be honest about his feelings if he was asking her to reveal hers. "Fifteen," he said, reciting the standard
lie. The age he'd been when the rest of the family had found
out. It wasn't that he didn't want to confide in her about dis-
covering his father with his mistress. He did. But tonight was
about getting past her issues, not his. "Old enough to understand and get really fucking angry and resentful," he said,
which was nothing short of the truth.

She nodded in understanding. "I was five when Mom died
and eight when my father remarried. I had eight years with
my dad, then my world changed. Another woman moved into
our apartment with her son, so my father immediately bought
a house because Janice wanted it. That meant Dad had to
take a second job to pay the mortgage. He wasn't around

anymore, only she was. And she had no patience for a needy little girl."

He curled his hands into fists, sorry he'd asked her to dig deeply into something that was going to cause her immeasurable pain. After all, he knew her father was in prison now. He'd never meant to hurt her by asking her to let him in, but he'd begun the discussion, so he had to listen to the rest.

"When Janice got sick, there was nothing he wouldn't do to help make her better, and I got pushed aside again, except this time I felt guilty for my thoughts because his wife was so sick."

Tyler thought he'd met her father in the hospital, but he'd been fifteen at the time. Not exactly paying attention. "And after your stepmom recovered? What happened then?"

"Once she was healthy, nothing my dad could give her was enough. She wanted to live. She left us, or should I say, she left him, and last I heard, she'd found herself a wealthy man who could keep filling her endless well of need."

Tyler nodded. "Then it was just the two of you again. You and your father."

"Yes. And I thought things would change, go back to the way they used to be before Janice. Except Dad was distraught over the breakup of his marriage and losing his wife. Once again, I was an afterthought." She pursed her lips and shrugged. "I wasn't enough to keep him from becoming a drunk or doing something dangerous and so incredibly stupid." She swiped at the tears in her eyes. "He's not worth it. But do you see now why I fall back into that way of thinking?"

"I do," he said, lifting her hand to his lips and brushing a kiss on her skin.

She visibly trembled at his touch but didn't pull back or away.

"I don't like that you automatically do it, and I hate that you lived it."

"You can't change the past," she said, never breaking eye contact, her breath uneven.

"No, but you can enjoy the present. We both can."

## Chapter Five

*E*lla wanted nothing more than to listen to Tyler, to relax and enjoy their time together, yet she couldn't help but wonder at his motives. What had shifted between them, and why was he suddenly interested in her after so much time keeping his distance?

Could she let that sublime kiss be her answer? Was he just finally giving in to an attraction that was very real—and always had been?

"You're overthinking again," Tyler said.

"You caught me." She let out a nervous laugh, unable to not be alarmed at the way he seemed to read her so well.

He slid his arm behind her on the couch and moved in closer, his warmth and body heat beckoning to her. "I know a way to make you stop worrying so much."

He was so serious, so intent on breaking down her defenses, and she was so tired of fighting herself and what she wanted.

She wanted Tyler.

She'd spent years running from her own sexuality after their night together. Maybe this was her opportunity to reclaim what she'd lost. This time she wasn't some starry-eyed teenage girl expecting him to fall head over heels in love with her after sex. She was an adult woman with needs he could fill, and maybe even help her get past the insecurities he'd instilled. Then when he inevitably moved on, and she knew he would, she'd be prepared and armed with the knowledge that this time, after Tyler, she'd be stronger. Not weaker.

Of course, she'd have to pretend she wasn't petrified of disappointing him in bed. She'd have to be like the girl who'd walked into his room, brave and determined.

She drew on every ounce of courage she had and met his blue-eyed gaze. Like everything else about him, his eyes were spectacular, pools of navy ink staring back, searching for . . . something.

Permission, she finally realized.

He wanted her consent before overwhelming her senses.

She rolled her shoulders back and took in his chiseled features—that determined, sexy expression—and prepared to dive in. He'd said he knew a way to make her stop worrying?

"What did you have in mind?" she asked, gliding her tongue over her bottom lip in a nervous gesture that had the blue in his irises deepening.

He slid a finger over the dampened spot she'd left behind. "I'm going to make sure you're too aroused to think," he promised as he released her lip and sucked his finger into his mouth, tasting her on his tongue.

She melted at his words, her sex softening and pulsing with need, her nipples beading into tight peaks. He was good, she thought, but then he'd never been the issue.

"I'm going to make damned sure you know that not only do I want to be with you, I need to be," he promised, leaning in and nipping at that same lip, causing a shock of electricity to light up inside her. "And this time you'll have no doubt afterward about how fucking good it was."

He followed up that statement by closing his mouth over hers. He'd primed her with his words, and she wanted this, wanted him, and opened for him without him even asking. He accepted her invitation, his tongue thrusting inside her parted lips. She moaned, and soon she was lost in sensation, in the glide of his lips. He didn't linger where he'd started, he slid his mouth lower, breathing warm kisses down her face, pausing to slide his tongue along her jaw, nibbling his way to her earlobe.

"You smell like coconut," he whispered, his breath hot and tantalizing against her skin.

"Sh-shampoo," she managed to get out, though she wasn't focused on anything but sensation and the male body pressing ever closer.

"Do you feel that?" he asked.

"What?"

"The heat." He nipped at her earlobe. "The anticipation." He tugged harder, and desire shot through her body. "We're combustible." As if to prove his point, he kissed her neck, an open-mouthed, wet kiss that had her nipples hardening beneath the cotton of her shirt.

He grazed his teeth across her shoulder and pulled the strap of her top with his teeth before releasing. "Have to get rid of this. I want to see those pretty breasts. My last glimpse was way too short."

She blushed at the reminder of her tank top slipping in their shared room on the island, but she was way too aroused to remain embarrassed for long. If his goal was to seduce her into calmness, he was succeeding, both with his words and his touch.

"You with me?" he asked.

She managed a nod, and without waiting, he lifted the hem of her top, pulling it up and over her head, leaving her in a flesh-toned bra decorated with white lace. He groaned, his eyes dilating as he stared at her chest.

Flustered by his intent gaze, she pulled her bottom lip between her teeth, and he shook his head. "Nobody bites that lip but me," he said in a commanding tone, more like the Tyler she'd come to know over the years than the one who'd been tiptoeing around the minefield she'd set up between them.

And she had to admit, if only to herself, it was hot as hell.

"Stand up," he said.

She blinked and rose to her feet, feeling led by him, almost as if she were in a trance. It worked for her, listening to his commands, not having time to think, and she sensed he knew it too.

"First I'm going to take that bra off and look at you."

He was looking now, she thought, her body tightening as he, too, stood and walked behind her. He brushed her hair off her shoulders, letting his calloused fingertips trail along her skin, goose bumps rising in the wake of his touch. He continued until he came to the back clasp of her bra and released the catch. Then, ever so gently and unlike his gruff orders, he slid the straps down her shoulders and arms until the garment fell to the floor.

She stood before him, her breasts exposed in a way she'd never experienced, but before her embarrassed or worried thoughts could surface, he strode around in front of her and cupped both mounds in his big hands. All rational thought fled; nothing but feeling and enjoyment remained. He palmed her breasts, pressing into her nipples with this thumbs, and the sensation went straight to her pussy, coating her panties with arousal.

"They fit perfectly in my hand," he said in a sexy growl. "Look."

She glanced down to see his tanned skin against her pale flesh. His hands were so big yet so soft as he kneaded her breasts and played with her nipples, clasping them between his thumb and forefinger, rolling them gently at first, then shocking her with a hard pinch to each tight bud.

She sucked in a stuttered breath, even more startled when the hint of pain morphed into heated pulses between her thighs. "More," she murmured, surprised when she heard her own voice.

He grinned and leaned down, sucking one nipple into his mouth, swirling it with his tongue, nipping with his teeth before releasing with a not-so-subtle pop. The sudden rush of cool air on her skin had her writhing where she stood, her empty body yearning for fulfillment.

"You like that," he said, his glittering blue eyes meeting hers.

"Feels like I do," she agreed, swaying on her feet.

"Stay with me," he said, bracing her with a hand on her shoulder. "Skirt off next."

"It's elastic," she said, wondering why she bothered explaining. His hands were already at the waist, hooking his thumbs into her panties and skirt, then yanking both down.

"Step out."

She was so aroused she was past embarrassment or concern. She just followed his orders and eased one foot, then the other out of the garment that joined the rest of her clothes on the floor.

He knelt at her feet, pulling her flip-flops off and discarding them as well. Then he grasped her ankle in one hand and glanced up—not to meet her gaze but to stare at her exposed sex, wet with her juices, pulsating with need.

She'd never—and she did mean never—ever let a man look at her this way. Dim lights, that was what worked for her. No criticism that way. No disappointment.

She was so lost in her own head she was startled when he leaned forward and bit lightly on her clit, shocking her back into sensory overload. She yelped at the sting, then shifted on her feet, moaning at the fire licking through her veins.

"Guess I have to keep things moving if I'm going to keep you here with me." He shot her a knowing, chastising look.

She managed a nod. "Guess so," she admitted, causing him to shake his head and laugh.

"I enjoy you, Ella."

Before she could answer, he picked her up as if she weighed nothing and headed toward the bedroom, carrying her over his shoulder. Uh-oh. They were really doing this.

No sooner did she have the thought than his hand came down solidly on her ass. She registered the smack of his hand and the shock of pain, and once again, ache turned into something else, something that had her moaning as desire floated her higher.

"No thinking," he said, easing her onto the bed, her back against her mound of pillows. "But yeah, we're really doing this," he said.

"How did you know what I was thinking?"

"You said it out loud," he said, shaking his head and laughing at the same time.

And wasn't that a sight, Tyler Dare, standing in her bedroom, grinning down at her while he unbuttoned his shirt. At that point, she had no problem letting her thoughts drift away as she studied the work of art that was his golden chest, sprinkled with dark hair that tapered into the waistband of his black jeans. He shucked the shirt, revealing sculpted, muscled abs and arms.

When she'd been with him last, he'd been young—hot, yes; chiseled from the army, definitely. But the man in front of her now was all grown up, defined in ways she'd yet to comprehend. He was gorgeous, and for the moment, anyway, he was all hers.

His hands came to his pants, and he worked open the button, repeating the process of removal just as he'd done with her, taking his underwear off along with the jeans. And then she lost her breath.

His erection was solid, proudly stretching out before her. There was no comparison. They'd been young, frantic, and all the work had been done under the covers. Now she could look her fill, and as she did, her body softened for him, a deep-seated yearning and need for him she'd kept hidden coming to the surface.

No! She desperately fought back the emotions that struggled to be released, because she'd always felt more for Tyler. But she couldn't afford anything beyond lust. Not this time. Not again.

Lust was safe, and she gave herself over to it, pushing herself back against the pillows and bravely spreading her legs. "Are you going to stand there? Or join me?" she asked.

An amused smirk lifted the corners of his mouth. "Do you think for one second you're in charge?"

Having let go of her emotional fears, at least for as long as this lasted, she bent one leg and stared up at him. "I'm not?" she asked cheekily.

"Not by a long shot," he said, his gloriously naked body finally covering hers.

She closed her eyes and drank him in, absorbing his heat, memorizing the feel of his legs tangled with hers, his chest hair abrading her sensitive nipples, the warmth of his lips against her cheek . . . and the strength and force of his erection pressing directly against her sex. Because she never knew if this would happen again, this time she wanted to forget fear and anxiety and memorize every last touch, stroke, and moment of being in his arms.

He reached up with one hand, grabbing a handful of pillows and tossing them to the floor, letting her head fall back against the mattress. "There." Bracing his hands on either side of her head, he levered himself over her, the only part of his body touching hers, his thick cock.

"Tyler," she moaned as his length drifted lazily back and forth over her clit, arousing her but not hard enough to take her where she wanted to go, which was up and over the edge she was riding.

"I fucking love hearing my name coming from that sexy mouth of yours," he said, closing his lips over hers and devouring her with a passion he'd been holding back.

He thrust his tongue inside her willing mouth and mimicked the sexual act she desperately desired while grinding his hips against hers, circling his groin over her clit, and finally allowing her to build toward a peak.

She arched her hips, meeting his moves and creating some of her own, every electrified glide of his erection spreading her juices over them both. She was breathing hard and could feel how quickly she was escalating toward climax. Waves started to pound at her, bring her close, so close, and suddenly he grabbed her hands, sliding them up and over her head.

He broke the kiss, stopped moving, and stared down at her intently.

"No," she cried out as the rush receded, leaving her empty and hanging. "Why did you stop?"

"Because when you have that orgasm, I'm going to be buried in that wet pussy of yours. So quick conversation."

Reality flooded back along with the embarrassing memories of the past.

*"Tell me you're on fucking birth control," Tyler said, his handsome face contorted with anger, and she scrambled to get away, fighting his body's hold on her and the fact that he wouldn't let her go.*

"Fuck," Tyler muttered, the sudden panic on Ella's face cluing him in that he'd crossed some line.

She squirmed beneath him, obviously desperate for escape, something he couldn't, wouldn't let happen. "Stop!" he said, trying his most commanding tone while bracing his legs over hers in an attempt to keep her beneath him.

She stilled, staring up at him, eyes not filled with desire as they'd been seconds earlier but a distinct wariness he'd put there.

"Talk to me," he said, capturing a tear as it dripped down her face by licking it with his tongue.

She smiled a little, something he counted as a win, but she immediately shut down again, her expression closed and tight. "You were about to ask about birth control, right?" she asked.

He nodded.

She met his gaze head on. "I know it's not like before, but last time you were so furious with me when you asked. I guess I flashed back and needed to get away."

In that instant, viewing the damage he'd done to her young psyche up close and personal, Tyler hated himself. But he couldn't change the past; he could only fix the future. "I screwed that up badly," he admitted. "But I need you to focus on the present, not the past. Can you do that?" Did she even still want to?

She blew out a shaky breath. "I can. And I'm still on birth control."

He knew what that truth cost her to say out loud. "Good." He brushed her damp face with his thumb. "I don't screw around all that often, and when I do, I use protection. That and I make sure to have a physical, so yeah. I'm clean. But the choice about a condom is up to you."

She studied his face as if searching for something. What, he didn't know, and in the wake of the silence, he heard himself continuing. "I never fuck without one, but I have to admit I want to feel your slick pussy coating my dick without protection. I want you to replace all those bad memories with new, fresh ones so you'll never doubt yourself again."

"Tyler." She said his name on a breathy moan, blinking up at him, those damp eyes suddenly glazing over again with desire. "I want that too," she admitted. "More than anything."

And that made him feel like a fucking king. He'd conquered their painful past and her fears. He didn't kid himself that her trust would last—her issues went too deep for a quick fix—but he'd keep her here in bed, and that's all he wanted for right now.

"And I promise I'm safe too."

He never had any doubt. Now he had to bring her back to a state of such extreme need that she wouldn't think anymore, only feel. He leaned down and pulled one nipple into his mouth, swirling the tip around, grazing with his teeth, until she was writhing beneath him. Her hips moved in endless circles, her slick moisture coating his cock.

Her hips jerked, and she grabbed his shoulders, her nails digging into his skin, marking him. Branding him. He wanted nothing more than to thrust up and inside her, and from her frantic moans and the way she thrashed beneath him—from nipple play alone—he had her back where he wanted her.

He leaned back and took his cock in his hand, pumping from base to tip. Precum coated his dick and fire raced through his body. Holding on, he rubbed his erection over her clit, tapping hard, his gaze alternating from her pussy to her face, contorted in ecstasy, and she was only partially there. He intended to take her the rest of the way.

"You ready, sweet girl?"

She bent her knees, a low moan escaping her throat.

"I'll take that as a yes. Keep your eyes on me. I want you to see my face as I take you."

Pretty hazel eyes locked on his, glazed and eager. That was the look he'd memorize and keep with him when they were apart.

"This is me, wanting you," he said, easing his cock into her tight sex. "Needing you." He pushed in farther, careful with her body and even more protective of her heart. "Not regretting a thing," he said, taking her completely.

Her slick walls clamped around him tightly, cushioning him in heat, pulsing with desire. For him. He forced his gaze to focus and caught the light in her eyes as he slid out and back in, harder and deeper with each thrust.

"Tyler, God. Again." She bent her knees and locked her legs around his back, pulling him so deep he saw stars. Like a teenager, he wasn't going to last, and he didn't give a shit as long as he took her over with him.

She cried out as he pounded into her, and he accepted her cries, swallowing them with his mouth. Breathing her in. Owning her. Changing him forever.

Because sex was easy. Sex, at least until now, didn't involve a lot of thinking about the other person's feelings. It was physical and led to mutual pleasure and needed release. This wasn't sex. With Ella, it was more. He felt it in his gut and in his core.

He slammed home, grinding himself against her sex, over and over, her soft cries growing louder, causing his body to tighten and grow ever harder. His balls drew up, his brain shorted out, but somehow he held off as she clawed at his shoulders and her body convulsed around him. He pulled muscles in his arms and shoulders waiting not only for her to finish but so he could change positions, shift his hips, and bring her to climax a second time.

Only then did he let go, allowing his orgasm to consume him, burning him from the inside out. He spilled himself inside her, losing himself to her soft body and warm heart.

Ella could barely catch her breath. She'd never had such fabulous, explosive sex before in her life. She'd never felt as though she were the center of someone's world before either. If his goal had really been to replace those bad memories, he'd done a damn good job.

She shivered and was grateful when Tyler rolled off her with a satisfied groan, afraid she'd get too used to his big body cushioning hers in all that heat and comfort.

He propped himself up on one arm and met her gaze. "So, didn't suck, did it?" he asked, a sexy, self-satisfied grin on his face.

And despite all the fears running through her brain, she couldn't help but laugh out loud. He'd done the impossible, breaking through the tension she'd no doubt have put between them.

"No, it definitely didn't suck," she agreed.

He reached out and twisted a strand of hair around his finger, tugging lightly on her scalp. Tingling awareness woke up her body all over again. Oh, he was addicting, she thought.

"I'm going to want to do that again. Soon."

"Is that so?"

"Any objections?" he asked, his voice a deep rumble.

She shook her head at his easy acceptance of something she was still struggling with. No matter how much she told herself this was sex for the sake of sex, with Tyler, it was always something more. But he'd told her going in, this was about replacing memories. It wasn't about a relationship . . . and she was okay with that. Because she needed the boost being with him gave her. And maybe when they parted ways this time, she would be more sexually secure and ready to move on.

He pulled at her hair, stinging her scalp. "You're thinking again."

"I am."

"Well, don't. Just be." He yanked her in closer and closed his lips over hers, sliding his tongue into her mouth the way he'd slid his thick erection into her sex. Giving up the fight, she moaned and plastered her body against his, kissing him back for all she was worth.

He cupped the back of her head in his hand and tilted her head, giving himself deeper access to her mouth. She loved how he kissed, possessing her, owning her, staking a claim, leaving her with no doubts of how much he desired her, uninhibited in his passion.

She hooked a leg over his and pulled herself against him, rubbing her pussy against his cock, which had begun to harden all over again. She appreciated his stamina as she rocked her hips in circles, bringing herself to a higher and higher peak.

He eased back and drew in a shallow breath, diving back in with long licks of his tongue along her jaw and neck. All the while, she arched herself against him as he met her need with rough, shaky thrusts of his hips, grinding himself against her. His erection rubbing against her clit, the friction so hot and good.

"I'm so close," she said on a groan, sensation coming at her from all sides.

"That's it, let go, sweet girl. Come all over me."

And she did, her body reacting to his words, to the exquisite feelings they created together. She cried out his name, unable to hold back, her orgasm a mind-blowing, earth-shattering experience, only marred by the fact that her body was still aching for him to fill her.

As if reading her mind, he caught the tail end of her climax, shifting their positions and thrusting up inside her. He hit her G-spot immediately, and she screamed, digging her nails into his shoulders as he continued to take her higher, slamming into her harder and harder.

Her orgasm seemed to go on, meeting his as he climaxed, his warmth bursting inside her. She didn't remember her orgasm ending, merely gasping for breath as Tyler slowly pulled out, leaving her empty.

But he didn't leave.

He merely pulled her into his arms, hooked a leg around her, and fell fast asleep.

A little while later, the distinctive buzz of a cell phone pulled her from the best slumber she'd had in a while. Hot. She was so hot. She came awake, realizing she was covered by Tyler's big, warm body, and as uncomfortable as she was, sticky and sweaty, a big grin worked its way onto her lips. Because she'd had sex with Tyler twice now.

And it really hadn't sucked.

She nudged him with her hand.

"Hmm?" he asked, still not awake, if she had to guess.

"Your phone was going off," she said, poking him again.

"Sleeping," he muttered.

So he was a big grumpy teddy bear when he didn't want to wake up. Good to know, she thought, just as his phone went off again.

"Must be important," she said, continuing her campaign of finger-jabbing him until he was awake.

He rolled onto his back with a loud groan. "Whoever it is, it'd better be a fucking emergency," he muttered and dragged himself out of bed.

No shame whatsoever, he strode naked to her side of the mattress, where he'd left his jeans on the floor, and pulled his cell out of his pocket. She ogled his tight, bare ass, figuring if he was going to display it, she was damn well going to look.

"Oh crap. It's Scott." He fumbled with the phone and called his brother back, bringing the cell to his ear. "Hey, man, what's up?"

Ella continued to watch . . . and admire his lean torso, tanned skin, tousled hair, and handsome face. She couldn't believe she was here, in her bed, with him.

She bit down on her lip and before the first worrisome, negative, unworthy thought could pop into her head, she shut it down.

Avery had been through a lot of therapy to control her anxiety, and she'd taught Ella some of her strategies, one of those being closing things up in a box and packing it away. Ella had used that often over the years, to avoid thinking of her father in prison or the painful knowledge that he'd killed someone while driving drunk or how she'd been ignored as a child. Yes, she had a lot of skill packing those things away.

She realized now that maybe not dealing with her issues wasn't the best thing in the world . . . Tyler had pointed that out earlier. She tended to get down on herself without realizing it. But for now, if she wanted to enjoy him, she had to push all other thoughts aside. Had to.

"Meg's in labor," Tyler said, breaking into her thoughts. "I have to shower and get to the hospital."

Excitement leapt through her. "That's amazing!"

Scott and Meg had gotten together in an untraditional manner, with Meg already pregnant with someone else's baby. That someone else had turned out to be a dangerous psycho with deep-seated issues from birth. After some real danger, he was now out of Meg's life for good, and the baby was Scott's, in name and in truth. Nothing would change that.

"Go!" she said when Tyler remained in place, staring at her until she blushed and pulled the covers up over her bare breasts.

"Come with me."

She blinked in surprise. She was close with Avery, and she liked Meg a lot, but did she belong at the hospital? Wasn't it a family moment? And she wasn't really family . . .

Without warning, Tyler hefted her into his arms and tossed her over his shoulder. Apparently he liked playing caveman.

"Hey!"

"I told you, no thinking!" He smacked her lightly on the ass. Again.

"Where are we going?" she asked, half shrieking, half laughing, completely aroused from that one smack.

"To shower and get to the hospital. My brother's having a baby."

She could argue, probably should . . . but he'd ordered her not to think. She'd told herself the same thing earlier. So she'd shower with her hot man and not overthink.

# Chapter Six

*T*yler didn't know how he survived the shower with Ella, standing inside the small enclosure, their bodies close, water streaming over her breasts and stomach in rivulets. She'd never looked hotter, especially after the night he'd spent in her bed. She was a mixture of innocence and seductress, and when she let go, he knew he was accomplishing his goal, showing her sex between a man and a woman could be amazing. It was only in her more rational moments that she doubted herself.

Which meant he still had more work to do. A good thing, since he wasn't finished with that sexy body. He'd only had a taste, hadn't nearly had his fill of all things Ella.

In the meantime, he was about to become an uncle, and he couldn't wait to see his brother, the one he was closest to, become a father. Tyler admired Ian, but he was more like the father figure that had replaced the one he'd lost. Scott was his partner and closest friend. And Tyler knew for damned sure Scott would be a better dad than they'd ever had.

They walked into the waiting room to find everyone was already gathered, except Avery, who'd left for LA with Grey and who, Tyler knew, was going to be upset she was missing the event. Even if she'd known it might happen.

At the very least, he and Ella would avoid Avery and her endless questions about why they were together.

On the big center sofa sat Tyler's mom, Emma, and her fiancé, Michael Brooks. Ian and Riley were standing in the back of the room, though they'd obviously left their three-year-old daughter, Rainey, at home. And a very pregnant Olivia and her husband, Dylan, sat in side-by-side chairs. Olivia was due in a month and a half, and she looked uncomfortably ready.

"Anything yet?" he asked, as if everything were normal and he and Ella hadn't strode in like a couple.

"Scott said he'd come out when he had something to report," Ian said from his stand by the window.

Riley waved at them from across the room.

His mother rose from her seat. Dressed immaculately as usual, in white slacks and a pale blue blouse, her hair pulled back with a clip and a hint of makeup on her face, she strode over.

They'd all been caught by surprise this morning, and now they waited for the newest Dare to join the family.

"Tyler." His mother kissed his cheek and pulled him into a hug.

"Hey, Mom." He hugged her back.

"Ella, so good to see you." Emma's bright eyes were sparkling with delight. "It's so right that you'd be here for such an important family event."

And leave it to his mother to make her feel welcome, Tyler thought gratefully.

"Hi, Emma. Thank you," Ella murmured.

"Well, come find a seat. It could be a while." She gestured to the room full of Dares.

"I hope nobody else is having a baby because there's no room for their families," Tyler said.

"We do take up a lot of space." Emma laughed and walked back to her fiancé, easing herself down beside him.

"Hey, you two, join us," Dylan said.

Olivia nodded in agreement. "Come take my mind off my own discomfort and talk to me."

"You're not feeling well?" Ella asked her.

Her husband placed a hand on her stomach. "It's just the six weeks. She's uncomfortable." He glanced at her in concern. "That's all it is, right? Because we are in the hospital."

"No, no. It's nothing urgent. Normal. Braxton Hicks contractions and all that. Can we stop talking about me?" she asked.

"Good idea," Ian said, joining them, Riley by his side. "Let's talk about you two. Run into each other in the parking lot?" he asked pointedly.

Tyler ignored him.

"Umm . . ." Ella fumbled for words.

"Leave them alone," Riley chided. "Just sit down." She pointed to a chair, and Ella gratefully escaped into it.

Next thing he knew, the women and Dylan were having their own private conversation, leaving Ian to eye him warily. "So did you make your move?" he asked quietly, so the women couldn't hear.

"You and Scott been talking about me?" Tyler asked, annoyed that Scott had gone blabbing to Ian about their conversation earlier.

"Just looking out for you. That's never going to change," Ian said in his always commanding tone. "So . . . you and Ella?"

Tyler breathed out hard, knowing his brother meant well. "We're just hooking up," he whispered, the words churning in his gut because it felt like so much more.

Ian shook his head, as if he was disappointed in that answer. "If it counts for anything, I think you two could be good for each other."

"Thank you, Dr. Phil," Tyler muttered, slapping his brother on the back.

They all talked quietly together, eventually leveling off into pairs again. Ian took Riley to get food for Emma, who Michael took for air. Dylan insisted he and Olivia take a walk to ease the pain in her back.

Tyler grabbed Ella's hand and led her to a corner of the room, needing private time with her after the grilling by his brother. She seemed dazed, and he couldn't blame her. His family was intense on a normal day.

He lifted her chin in his hand, forcing her to meet his gaze. "You good?" he asked.

She blew out a long breath. "I forget how overwhelming your big family can be," she said on a shaky laugh.

"The girls giving you a hard time?" he asked.

She shook her head. "Nothing I can't handle. It's girl talk. I've seen everyone on the other side at one point or another. I'm just not used to it being me."

He nodded, studying her for any signs of panic or withdrawal. Finding none, he let out a relieved breath and brushed his lips over hers. "Good. It'll get easier each time."

"You promise?"

"Swear," he said, kissing her more thoroughly, more deeply, but he maintained control, completely aware of where they were.

"Did I get here in time?" Avery's voice interrupted them, and Ella jerked out of his grasp. "I was about to board when I got the call," his sister continued.

Tyler swung around just after Avery burst into the room, out of breath. For Ella's sake, Tyler prayed his sister's mind remained on the new baby and not—

"What did I just walk in on?" Avery asked, her startled gaze jumping from Tyler to Ella. "Are you two hooking up?"

Ella cringed at getting caught kissing Tyler by his sister, her best friend. Given the choice, she'd want to sit Avery down and talk to her, explain both the past and the present. In fact, she'd planned on calling her as soon as she had a chance. Avery wasn't just her best friend, she was her sister. The person who'd stood by her when no one else had. She couldn't risk losing her.

"Avery—" Tyler began.

"Avery, please, can we talk?" Ella brushed past him and headed for her friend, determined to take charge of the conversation.

She glanced over Ella's shoulder to Tyler, then looked back to Ella. "Sure. I take it there's been no baby?"

"Not yet. Everyone took a break, but they'll all be back soon," Ella said She grasped Avery's hand and led her to the farthest chairs.

Tyler took a step toward them. Ella shook her head. "No. I need to talk to your sister."

He held up both hands and backed away, leaving the two women alone.

"Are you hooking up with my brother?" Avery asked, her voice tempered. Not angry, but not jumping for joy either. "I saw the chemistry between you two when you returned from the island. So?"

Ella shook her head and looked into her friend's concerned gaze. "You need to brace yourself because it's more than just the one night we just spent together." She twisted her hands together nervously.

"Relax and talk to me," Avery said.

Ella blew out a breath and stared up at the dingy hospital ceiling. Of all the places she thought she'd admit her youthful indiscretion, a hospital waiting room wasn't one of them. "Okay. Remember the Christmas we snuck the schnapps from behind your parents' bar and got drunk?"

Avery grinned and let out a laugh. "Of course I remember. I passed out cold so damned fast."

"And after you did, I . . . snuck into your brother's room."

Avery brushed back her bangs and blinked. Then blinked again. "You snuck into Tyler's room?"

Ella nodded. "And into his bed."

Her friend's eyes opened wide. "Did you . . . ?"

Again, Ella nodded.

"But you were a virgin!" Avery shouted . . . just as the rest of the family filed into the room. "Sorry," she muttered.

The rest of them gave Ella and Avery a wide berth, so Ella figured she might as well continue. "Yes, I was a virgin."

"You . . . Tyler . . . He took your—" A bright flush stained Avery's cheeks. "Oh my God."

"I didn't tell you because I was ashamed. Ashamed of what I did under your mother's roof, ashamed of how I acted, that I betrayed your trust." She trembled as she relived those awful feelings, feeling so pained at having betrayed her friend. "And things didn't end well between me and Tyler afterward, which was another part of the reason I wanted to put the whole sordid thing behind me."

Avery twisted her fingers together, obviously thinking hard about what she'd just heard. "So . . . that's why things between you two were always so weird."

"Yeah." Among other reasons, including what he'd said to her afterward, but Ella didn't need to share the details. She only needed Avery to know she was sorry.

"And now?" Avery asked.

"Now . . . we're sort of . . . hooking up."

"I see."

"If it's going to come between us, you know—"

Avery put her hands over Ella's, stilling the nervous movement. "What you do with Tyler has nothing to do with me. It's just that . . ." She paused and drew a deep breath. "My brother is a player. Not that he's always with a woman, far from it," she rushed to explain. "It's just that from all I've seen over the years, he doesn't do commitment. In fact, it's a pattern of his. A date or two and he's out."

Ella ignored the pain in her heart caused by hearing what she already knew to be true. "I'm aware that whatever's going on between us is temporary." Get her sea legs back when it came to sex and move on. She could handle it. She had no choice.

"Okay, good. Because if he hurts you, I'll have to kill him, and he's my brother, you know?" Avery met her gaze with a serious expression on her face.

"I know. And I appreciate the support. But you don't have to worry. I'm not stupid enough to think I can change him." Although Ella knew many other women might think they were the one to change a bad boy's ways, Ella knew better. She hadn't been enough . . . for a lot of things in her short life.

She didn't consider this kind of thinking to be what Tyler had accused her of earlier: selling herself short. No, she considered it realistic. Smart. More of a honing of her survival skills, she thought wryly. "You don't need to worry about either one of us. We're adults and we'll behave like it before and after."

"You're sure?" Avery asked, chewing on her bottom lip.

Ella didn't want her friend worrying. She leaned in and hugged Avery hard. "You worry too much. It's all good."

"Okay," Avery said, but Ella wasn't sure her friend believed her own words.

Before she could figure out what to do or say next, Scott stepped inside the waiting room, a big grin on his face. "It's a boy," he announced, pumping a fist in the air.

Ella grinned, happy for Meg and Scott, who'd gone through so much to be together.

If she thought the Dares were excitable normally, nothing topped a baby coming into the family. The noise and cheers, the crying and phone calls were overwhelming.

The family took turns going into the room so as not to overwhelm the new parents. Emma and Michael went in first, then Olivia and Dylan, followed by Ian and Riley.

By the time they came out, Avery was bouncing on her feet in the excitement that vibrated through the room. "You go in with Avery," Ella said to Tyler. "I'll be here when you get out." She didn't mind seeing the baby at their home, once they were settled in.

Tyler shook his head. "Avery, go on in. I'll wait and go with Ella when you're done," Tyler said, taking Ella by surprise, but she appreciated the gesture, especially once they walked into the room and she caught sight of the gorgeous little boy swaddled in a blanket and snuggled in his mother's arms.

"Oh, he's darling," Ella said.

"You did good," Tyler said to Meg. He then turned to his sibling. "I'm happy for you, man." He slapped his brother on the back.

Scott scooped the baby out of his wife's arms. "Want to hold him?" he asked Tyler.

Tyler immediately settled into a chair, and Scott handed him the baby. "His name is Cole," Scott said.

Tyler glanced down at the tiny baby in his arms, and Ella could swear her ovaries sang. Her heart definitely grew in size. Everything about him softened when he looked down at the tiny bundle and grinned.

"Hey, little man. Don't you worry about getting him as your father. Uncle Tyler's going to teach you all you need to know about the important things in life." He stroked his big hand down the baby's soft cheek and hummed a little.

He looked so right with the baby, and if she let herself, she could see it. See Tyler and his own baby—their—

Before she could finish the thought, Tyler looked up. He met and held her gaze, a heavy thread of emotion and the baby between them.

Panicked suddenly, unwilling to want or even think about what she couldn't have, Ella cleared her throat. "I'll meet you outside," she said to Tyler. "Meg, Scott, congratulations. I wish you every happiness." She treated them to a brief wave and rushed out the door, leaving her feelings, and her useless hopes and dreams, behind.

While holding his nephew, the smell of baby powder in his nose, Tyler had a flash. It only lasted for a second, but it was long enough for him to catch sight of Ella watching him with the infant, her eyes soft and dewy. And in that instant, he thought, this could be us. And his heart nearly stopped beating.

Because permanency, family, none of that was in his future. Unless he believed he could commit. And he just wasn't ready. He didn't trust himself yet. Wasn't sure he ever could, and that was starting to scare the hell out of him, the knowledge that he'd end up alone, lose the best thing in this lifetime, and he'd have only himself to blame.

Shaken, Tyler said good-bye to his brother and his sister-in-law and brushed his lips over the baby's delicate forehead, kissing his nephew good-bye.

He met up with Ella back in the waiting room. The rest of the family had gone home. He walked in and his gaze locked with hers. Despite the feelings that tormented him, he was drawn to her nevertheless. Her wide-eyed honesty, the independence he wanted to conquer and yet never take away. And her vulnerability—he'd seen the occasional haunted look in her eyes when surrounded by his family, the realization of what she lacked in her life, and the notion that he would give her all those things, if only he were capable.

Dammit. He needed to stop thinking. "Ready to head out?" he asked.

She picked up her purse from one of the chairs. "I am. It's almost one in the morning," she said on a yawn.

He drove them back to her place, both of them keeping the quiet peace, lost in their own thoughts. He intended to walk her inside and say good night. Too many emotions had pummeled him, and it was safer to just go home.

He parked, and they took the elevator up to her apartment. Unable not to touch her, he placed a hand on the small of her back, feeling the heat of her skin through the thin top she wore, committing it to memory.

She paused at the door and pulled out her keys. "I know it's late," she said, turning to face him. "But I was wondering if you wanted to . . . come in," she offered, her hazel eyes warm and inviting.

And though he knew what he ought to do, he found himself nodding in agreement instead. If he could suppress his emotions, lose the feelings he had for her in physical release, then just maybe he could get his head back on straight. At the same time, he reminded himself what he'd offered her. Sex to replace the bad memories he'd given her in the past with good ones for the future.

Sex for sex's sake.

Yeah, right. He was frustrated with himself and his inability to stick to the rules he'd set out, and annoyed with his fucking emotions, which he'd never asked to come into play.

But they had, and he didn't want to think anymore. He wanted to lose himself in Ella. No sooner did she shut the door behind her than he had her against the wall, his lips against hers, her sweet scent permeating his pores, devastating his senses.

And she held on as he devoured her mouth, taking everything she had to give. And she gave plenty, kissing him back, pulling at his hair, and grinding her hips against his until his cock was hard as stone. He had no patience or time for finesse or foreplay, and from the way she writhed against him, she lacked interest in any teasing as well.

For him, nothing would do except burying himself inside her hot, wet heat.

He tore his mouth from hers, gasping for breath. Hooking his arm around her waist, he led her across the room to the edge of the couch. She was still panting by the time they reached their destination.

He pulled her top up and over her head, taking a moment to admire the view of her ripe, plump breasts and hardened nipples before yanking down her skirt, removing her panties with shaking hands. And that had never happened before—him being so affected by a woman he trembled like a teenager with his first crush.

Shaken by the continued depth of his feelings, he spun her away from him and bent her over the edge of the sofa, running his hands down the smooth globes of her ass. She moaned at the caress, and he squeezed each cheek harder. She wriggled her ass beneath his touch.

All the while, he continued to stroke her, gliding his fingertips between her cheeks, into the silken wetness of her sex. Her moisture coated his fingertips, causing his body to tighten even more. He spent a few long, delicious minutes stroking her pussy, sliding his fingers along the outer lips of her sex, reveling in her hot moans and sighs. She even arched her back, angling her ass farther upward, giving him deeper access, and he slid a finger into her slick heat.

"Oh, Tyler," she said, voice low and throaty, as he pumped one digit in and out of her tight channel, all but fucking her with his finger.

She clamped her body around him, and he nearly came in his pants like a fucking boy instead of a man who could control himself and his baser needs. Except this was Ella, and when it came to her, Tyler had no goddamned control.

He slid his finger out, and her body trembled from head to toe. He needed to be inside her now.

He leaned over her, brushing her hair off her back, his lips close to her ear.

"Do you feel empty without me?" he asked.

"So empty. I need you." She squirmed, clearly on the edge and so needy she ramped up his desire to unrivaled proportions.

He shucked his jeans and briefs, kicking them aside, and slid a hand over his dick, pumping back and forth, praying he would last beyond that first hot thrust.

He braced a hand on her lower back. "You ready, sweet girl?" He followed up the question by sliding his cock along the seam of her ass, and she moaned out loud.

He'd take that as a yes. "Hold on, because this is going to be rough."

"Ohh, I hope so."

"You up for it?" he asked, needing to make sure. To hear the words.

"Oh yes," she said, pushing her ass back against his hard-as-nails erection.

At her eager response, he pressed her down into the couch. She raised herself up, indicating her readiness. Fuck, but her sweet ass was a sight to look at.

Sweating and on fire, his balls tight, his body ready to come, he took himself in hand and slid the head of his cock through her slick wetness, pushing upward, into her waiting heat, sliding all the way home, as her slick body sucked him in.

After that, it was as quick and dirty as he'd wanted it when he was determined to put all emotion aside and lose himself in sex. Just plain fucking sex. He thrust in and out, fast and hard, each drive harder and in time to her eager cries.

He'd never felt such ultimate perfection as her body, cushioning his, sucked him dry as he jerked his hips back and forth, losing himself in everything that was Ella.

"Oh God, oh God." She came, shuddering around him, bringing him nearer to his own climax.

As he drew closer to release, he realized the joke was on him. With Ella, it could never be plain sex. Not when she lit up his world in ways he didn't deserve.

But his body wasn't interested in facts, only in sensation. And nothing felt better as he let go, spilling himself inside the woman he sensed could complete him.

Which was why, when everything was said and done, he kissed her good-bye and headed home, punishing himself by not spending the night.

Ella woke up sore and sexually satisfied. It should have been enough. She wanted it to be enough. After all, she'd come screaming, harder than she ever had in her life. But then he'd dressed, claimed it was late, and left for the night. The same man who'd hooked his leg around hers and slept curled around her so she felt like she was in an oven the night before.

Lesson learned, she thought, ignoring the lump in her throat. Apparently he'd meant what he'd said. He wanted her. He'd replace her bad memories with good. And she could count on him to keep his word. All good to know. She just wouldn't invest her heart in him again. And how frustrating was it that she needed to constantly remind herself of something she already knew?

Because despite her independent streak, she wanted someone who loved her unconditionally. She'd never experienced that in her life. Not even with family. Especially not with family. Which led her to wonder why Tyler, who, despite his father's betrayal, had a close-knit family who would never abandon him, couldn't manage to find it in himself to commit.

Well, she wasn't the one who was going to change him. So time to move on with her own life. For the next few days, she fell back into a routine. She headed into work early. Ella had a stack of phone calls to make, including following up with the factory for the spring line and confirming recent orders. Not to mention Angie had left a stack of magazines on the desk for her to go through.

From Ella's desk, she heard Angie on the phone, her voice loud and clearly agitated. "Well, I don't care. You need to find a buyer. You assured me before the purchase it wouldn't be an issue. Just do it!" she said, slamming down the receiver.

Ella cringed and kept her eyes on her desk, which was a good thing, since Angie stormed out of her office a second later, grumbling about incompetent idiots. Without a word, she slammed paperwork on Ella's desk and headed back into her office. Angie was prone to blowups when things didn't go her way, so Ella ignored the tantrum, knowing it wasn't directed at her. She glanced at the documents, fully understanding what she needed to do, and got back to work.

She worked late the next two days, catching up. The following evening after work, she met up with a friend, Jillian Novak, who was an assistant for a shoe designer, also based out of Miami. They often went to trade shows and fashion exhibitions together. Jillian was in a long-term relationship with her boyfriend from high school, and since he was traveling, she'd asked Ella if she wanted to go out for dinner.

By the time she walked into the Japanese restaurant, Ella's mood had gone from cautiously optimistic about things with Tyler, despite his quick disappearing act, to feeling completely let down. She didn't expect to see him constantly, nor did she think he had to be in touch daily, but three days and she'd received one vague text:

Have to head out of town on business for two days and fully booked with meetings and a dinner the day I return. Will get in touch.

Although it wasn't fair to Tyler considering he'd lived up to everything he'd promised, she had one word for how she felt.

Used.

The text seemed like a nice blowoff. After she'd gone with him to the hospital to see his brother's new baby and later he'd bent her over the sofa and fucked her brains out, he'd all but disappeared.

"Men," she muttered, sliding into a chair across from her friend.

Jillian, a pretty redhead with blue eyes and long spiral curls, looked at her with concern. "What happened?"

"Let's just say I really don't know how to play the game." Ella gestured to the waiter and ordered a white wine spritzer, needing a little fortification and buzz to take the edge off her emotions.

"Love isn't a game." Jillian took a sip of her vodka tonic, her usual drink of choice.

"No, but sex is, and that's all I signed up for. I just realized it's hard for me not to feel disappointed when the guy can't be bothered to call and sends one line of text instead." She shrugged and glanced at the hardback menu, not really seeing what was listed before her.

"Don't sweat it. You'll find the right guy who will appreciate all you have to offer."

"I'm really not sure I'd recognize him if I did."

"Can I take your order?" the waiter stepped up to the table and asked.

Ella met Jillian's gaze. She nodded and rattled off some specialties from the menu.

The man turned to Ella, who settled for the basics: a California roll, a Philadelphia roll, and edamame. She wasn't all that hungry. And she was unsure if she was more upset with Tyler for disappearing or with herself for (a) expecting more than he'd promised and (b) for caring.

Because if she didn't care, she couldn't be hurt. And she'd promised herself she wouldn't let Tyler Dare hurt her again.

# Chapter Seven

*T*yler had a security job out of town, a high-profile client who insisted he be there in person to handle the details. He worked long hours and arrived home in time for his monthly dinner with Serena and her six-year-old daughter, JayJay, named after her father, Jack Junior. They always met at her favorite place, Pizza Palace, where they gave her dough to play with at the table.

He arrived to find the ladies already seated. No sooner had he walked over than JayJay jumped up squealing. "Uncle Tyler!" The words came out more like a shriek at high decibels than a normal tone.

"Hi, babycakes!" He leaned in, and she braced her dough-covered hands on his cheeks and treated him to a sloppy kiss.

"Hi, Serena." He sat down in the chair next to JayJay, across from Serena.

"Hi." She picked up a napkin and dipped it in a glass of water, leaned across, and wiped his cheek. "Sorry."

He shook his head. "It's fine. She's happy to see me."

"You're so good with kids," Serena said, her brown eyes warm as she glanced at her daughter.

Her words gave him pause. "You think so?"

He had his niece, Rainey, a three-year-old with her mother and father's independent streak. He spent time with her at every family gathering, remembered to bring a gift, usually a unicorn since she was obsessed with the mythical creatures, and he'd even been known to make up a story or two for her amusement.

He set a stuffed dog he'd been holding beneath his arm in front of JayJay. "Puppy!" she yelled, causing her mother to whisper about using her indoor voice. Serena had been putting off dog requests from the precious child, and Tyler thought it was his duty to provide substitutes for the time being.

"Of course I think you're good with her. You show up every month. It means the world to her. And to me." Serena pushed her brown hair off her shoulders.

"I love you guys. Besides, if Jack can't be here, I can." He glanced at JayJay, who didn't react to the mention of her father's name. She was absorbed in play, babbling at her new stuffed toy.

"Don't worry. She doesn't remember him," Serena said sadly. "Though I do talk about him often. Once she's older, I want her to know about her dad. Although I think I could live without her ever finding out he ran away from base camp in Iraq and went AWOL and was killed by the enemy." She shook her head, and he placed his hand over hers.

"I haven't come to terms with it either," Tyler said. "I just wish—"

"What?"

He took another look at JayJay, who'd turned to pounding the pizza dough. She looked so much like her father a lump rose to his throat.

"I wish I'd realized he was serious. All those times he talked about just walking away." Tyler ran a shaking hand through his hair. "I mean, we all talked about it. Joked about it, really. What else could we do in that hellhole of IEDs and women and children willing to blow themselves up?" He cut himself off and muttered a curse at his callous words in front of Jack's widow and child.

This was why he didn't talk about his time there. He hadn't been in Iraq long, though the year had felt like forever, and he'd come away damned lucky. Just horrific dreams and memories he'd never forget. And he hadn't experienced as much horror as many of the guys. But the sounds, the screams, the fear that any drive or step could be your last remained with him.

And now he was screwing this up in front of Jack's family.

"Tyler, no. How could you have known Jack would just . . . slip out one night?"

He glanced at the paper-covered table. Crayons from JayJay surrounded him as did scribbles that were on his side too. "He was my best friend. I should have seen it was more than just words. And maybe I did see and didn't want to because then I'd have had to do something. Like report him to my superior, and he'd have been so fuck—so angry." Like he hadn't told his mother about finding his father and his mistress.

Pain sliced through his chest at both remembrances. So many *if onlys* . . .

Serena toyed with a fork in front of her, spinning it between her hands. "I honestly don't think any decision you made under those conditions could have been the wrong one. Unless you weren't there for him when he needed you, and I know you were."

Tyler let out a low, sarcastic laugh. "You're so sure."

"I am." She glared at him for questioning her.

"How? How do you know?" he asked, for reasons beyond Jack and even beyond the choices he'd made after finding his father.

He was asking because, after three days apart, he couldn't stop thinking about Ella. Wanting to talk to her. To hear her laugh. To have her argue with him. Hell, he'd even take her insisting she could handle herself as long as she was near.

He wanted desperately to see if he and Ella could try for something more than just sex. Something solid. And to do that, he needed to believe in himself.

Serena braced her elbows on the table and leaned forward. "I know because you've been there for me and JayJay since the day you came home. Just like you're there for your siblings no matter what. And the business you created so you, me, and the guys you served with could have jobs when their tours were up. You're a good man, Tyler. I just don't know why you doubt yourself so much."

She stunned him with her words and her faith—with facts he'd never considered before—and allowed him to think that maybe he was no longer the same person who ran when things got emotionally hard. Maybe running wasn't really what he'd done, just made youthful choices? Done the best he could at the time?

"Ready to order?" the waiter, who Tyler hadn't even noticed, asked.

"Pizza!" the precious six-year-old said, and both Tyler and Serena laughed, breaking the tension.

And after they ordered, and while they ate, they talked about JayJay's friends, school, and the doggie she wanted that her mother wasn't at all ready to get. All the while, Serena's words stayed with him, as did thoughts of Ella and his desire to see her again.

But after three days and her lack of reply after he'd texted her, he had a feeling he'd screwed up somehow. He wasn't sure exactly how.

Before he could decide whether or not to run his personal issues by Serena, his phone rang with the business ringtone. He held up a hand to excuse himself for a minute. "Hello?"

"This is central station. You asked to be notified if anything came in on 2020 Mercer Street," the person on the other end said.

Ella's apartment, which had been his sister's place. Tyler had put the alarm system in when Avery had had a stalker, courtesy of her rock star (then-)boyfriend.

"I did. What happened?" Tyler asked.

"The alarm went off, indicating someone tried to break in. No one answered when we called, and the police were dispatched to the scene."

"Thank you." Tyler's entire body tightened with a combination of anger and frustration with himself for ignoring his gut on the island.

He glanced at Serena, rising as he spoke. "I have to go. It's an emergency."

"What's wrong?" she asked.

He kissed her on the head. "I wish I had time. I'll explain later. Just don't worry." He bent down and ruffled JayJay's hair. "Be good. I'll see you soon."

"Bye, Uncle Tyler."

He grinned. "Bye, babycakes."

He pulled money out of his pocket, causing Serena to frown. "You pay me well enough to cover a pizza dinner."

"It's always my treat. I'm sorry to run out," he said, then proceeded to do just that, hightailing it over to Ella's apartment and praying she was okay.

He arrived to find her talking to a police officer in the hall, a young guy who'd obviously been out on patrol when the call had come in about a possible burglary. His partner stood by his side.

Ella had her purse on her arm and wore a pretty sundress and heels. She'd obviously been out, just as he'd been, and gotten the call.

"Are you okay?" Tyler asked, coming up beside her.

"What are you doing here?" she asked, narrowing her gaze.

The officer stepped between them. "Is this a friend of yours?"

Ella hesitated, obviously annoyed with him. If she chose to get stubborn now, she'd cost the cops time because they'd start looking into him as a possible suspect. He waited for her to reply.

Finally she let out a huff of air. "Yes, he's a friend who thinks it's his job to watch out for me."

It was his turn to narrow his gaze. That kind of description wasn't going to fly.

The officer seemed to relax and stepped away.

Tyler went on to explain. "My sister used to rent this apartment too, and I put the security system in." Tyler reached into his pocket and slid a business card out of his wallet, handing it to the silent second officer. "I got the call from the alarm company because, as Ms. Shaw said, she's like family." He forced a smile for the other man's benefit. "Can you tell me what happened?"

The cop glanced at Ella, waiting for her okay to talk in front of him.

She nodded. "You can tell us both."

"There're signs of someone trying to break in," the cop said, pointing to jagged scrapes on the wall beside the door-knob and chipped paint around the dead bolt. "But the alarm must have scared them, and they ran. Not many people in these types of buildings have a security system. You're smart, Ms. . . ." He waited for her reply, pen in hand so he could write down pertinent information.

"Shaw. Ella Shaw," she said in a shaky voice.

"Ms. Shaw, is there a reason someone would target your apartment?"

She ran her hands up and down her forearms, making Tyler want to pull her into his arms and ease her stress. Except he knew she wouldn't be receptive, and he didn't want to cause trouble in front of the cop by pulling his protective routine. No police officer would appreciate his tactics.

"I don't know," Ella said. "I just returned from a business trip in St. Lucia, and I had . . . issues while I was there."

"What kind of issues?"

She told him about the mugging and her room being bro-ken into. Tyler didn't mention feeling that someone had fol-lowed them to the airport because he had no proof, only his gut instinct, which he'd stupidly ignored. He had a top-notch security staff he could use not only to protect her but to inves-tigate as well.

"What did the island police say?" the officer asked.

"Not much considering they were busy with a hurricane, and I left the island, but . . ." She trailed off and Tyler's nerves tingled in a way he did not like one bit.

"But what?" Tyler asked.

She bit on her nail, not meeting his gaze, further affirming his gut, which told him he wasn't going to enjoy what she had to say next. "I've had this weird feeling like someone's following me since I've been back."

"What?" The word exploded from him, and she flinched.

"Sir, if you don't calm down, I'll have to ask you to leave."

Tyler gnashed his teeth and nodded. "Ella, when were you going to mention that?"

She glanced up at him with those damned wide eyes that got to him every time. "I wasn't sure. And I didn't want to make a big deal if I was wrong. It was that first day after we got home. It's been quiet since then, so I put it out of my head."

"Miss, did you see anyone you could provide a description of?"

She swallowed hard. "Just a guy with dark hair. He was staring at me through a shop window. I kept busy, and when I looked again, he was gone."

"Did he look familiar to you?" the other cop asked.

"Was he the guy who mugged you?" Tyler pushed further.

She shrugged. "I didn't get a good look at the mugger. I know he had dark hair, but so do most men on the island and half the male population of Miami."

The cop flipped his notepad closed. "If you'd like to come downtown and file a report, we can at least have something official."

"I'll bring her down tomorrow," Tyler said. "She's shaken up now, and it's late."

"Will you be okay?" the second uniform asked. "We can drop you somewhere if you'd like."

"No. She'll be staying with me," Tyler said before Ella could reply.

"What? No, I'll be fine at home."

"We'll leave it to you to sort things out. If you need anything or remember any details, call." He handed her a card.

She took the paper and nodded. "Thank you."

Tyler waited for the two men to depart before turning to Ella.

"Don't start," she said, grabbing the doorknob. The door was already partially open from when she'd let the police inspect the interior. "I'm not in the mood to argue with you, so why don't you turn around and go home. I'll just set my alarm and be perfectly fine." She opened the door and attempted to slam it behind her, but he caught it with his hand, following her inside.

He wasn't leaving. "You're pissed. Why don't you tell me why."

She spun around to face him. "Because you're a man."

He couldn't suppress a grin. "Is that all?"

"It's not funny. Look, I realize we agreed to sex only, but a one-line text after everything we did together . . . well, I don't think . . . I'm not . . ."

"C'mere." He grabbed her hand and pulled her toward the sofa, feeling her resistance the entire way. He wasn't deterred. At least now he knew how he'd fucked up.

"I was in Colorado doing work for a client. Between the time change and the way he insisted on overseeing the project, I didn't have any time to myself. That said, I was an ass. I should have made the time to call. It's not like I wasn't thinking about you, because I was. And it's sure as hell not like I didn't want to see you when I came home, but I have a monthly dinner with Serena and her daughter, and I didn't want to disappoint the kid."

"And I wouldn't want you to."

"Texting works for a guy."

She shot him a death glare. "It doesn't for women."

"Noted. Now when were you going to tell me you were being followed?"

Ella knew it was too good to be true when she thought she could pretend this whole nightmare wasn't happening. Why would anyone be after her? She couldn't come up with one single reason.

"I really thought it was residual anxiety from the mugging," she said, still surprised that Tyler was here and trying not to read too much into it.

After all, he'd said he'd gotten a call from his alarm company. He'd also said he'd wanted to talk to her, to see her . . .

"Okay, well, I think we can safely assume it wasn't anxiety or imagination. Now pack your things. You're coming with me," he said, stepping ever closer as he spoke.

Whoa. Hello. "You can't show up here, giving me orders."

He raised an eyebrow in that cocky way of his, the one that gave him extra sex appeal. "Want to bet?"

"Oh no. No lifting me up and carrying me anywhere," she said, figuring out what he meant because he'd done it before.

"Then pack up your things." He hesitated before adding, "Please."

She blew out a long breath. "To go where? And why?"

He took her hand, surprising her by running his thumb back and forth over her skin. "To a hotel for the weekend."

He rendered her speechless and took advantage by continuing before she could gather her wits and argue.

"We've been going at this all backward, upside down, and crazy. Sex, then silence . . . I want to spend time together. To talk and just get to know each other apart from family and the insanity of someone obviously out to get you. And while we're gone, I'll get my men to investigate your life and see who could be after you and why."

He might as well have picked her up and tossed her over his shoulder, her head hanging down, because she was dizzy from his proclamation. She tried to process it all, from him wanting to take her away for the weekend to spend time together to his point about investigating her life to the seductive brush of his fingers over her skin.

"So what do you say?" he asked, his tone all low and sexy.

"I have a choice?" she asked.

"Goddammit," he muttered. "Are you for real?"

A grin played around the edges of her mouth because, whether he knew it or not, he had her.

His hot gaze settled on her lips. "You're joking," he said, his shoulders dropping in obvious relief.

"I am."

But just because she agreed didn't mean her stomach wasn't twisting with nerves over spending a weekend alone with Tyler. Then again, if she mentally took herself back to the mind-set of an affair and ignored her annoying emotions, which had driven her crazy over the last few days, she ought to be fine.

"I'll come with you. Because this time you asked me nicely, and also because I'm not stupid and getting out of here is the smart thing to do," she said.

He nodded. "I'm going to want a list of everyone in your life, from your boss's full name to those of the others who work with you and your friends'. Nobody is off-limits until I figure out what's going on. But let's focus on work first, since this started while you were away on business."

She sobered at the thought. "My boss? Angie's eccentric and demanding, but she'd never hurt me." She looked down, saddened by the very thought.

He rested his knuckles beneath her chin, tipping her head up to meet his gaze. "I'm not going to take any chances. There have been too many incidents."

She nodded, knowing he was right. So without argument, she headed into her bedroom, pulled out a bag, and packed up her suitcase. Not knowing what he had in mind, she chose a variety of outfits, bathing suits, cover-ups, and restaurant-type wear. She kept a packed cosmetic bag with toiletries since she traveled for work, and added a few more items she used daily.

She tried not to think about what this weekend meant. She'd go with him, she'd be safe, and that was that. She hoped.

A few minutes later, she met Tyler back in the living room, rolling her suitcase behind her.

He stood at the window, his hands in his pants pockets, pulling the material tight over his spectacular behind. She bit her bottom lip in an attempt not to comment on the fact that she wanted to squeeze him tight with both hands and never let go.

She cleared her throat instead. "All set."

He turned to face her, glancing at his wristwatch. "I'm impressed."

"I thought you might be."

"Ready?"

As I'll ever be, she thought, and she nodded. "Where are we going?"

"While you were packing, I called a friend who owns a boutique hotel on Ocean Drive near the Art Deco District. Only eighteen rooms. Totally peaceful and secluded. He always keeps a room available for a friend in need."

"Nice," she murmured. "What's the name?"

"La Belle. It's named after his wife," he said, taking the suitcase out of her hand.

"That's incredibly romantic." She turned to set the alarm, not wanting him to see what was probably a wistful look on her face at the story of a man naming a hotel after the woman he loved. "Don't you need to pick up things to wear?" she asked him, forcing her mind to more practical matters.

"I have a change of clothes in the car that I keep for when I go to the gym, and I can buy anything else I need," he said, as if it was that simple. And she supposed it was.

A few minutes later, they set off in his Range Rover, headed to South Beach, where the hotel was located. He called Luke Williams, one of his security men. Tyler explained Ella's situation and what he needed from the man, who then peppered Ella with questions about her life so he could begin looking into why someone was targeting her. Tyler directed the conversation, the main focus being on her job, her boss, and anyone she'd worked with regarding the photo shoot before and during their time on St. Lucia, since that was where the first incident had occurred. Luke promised to put eyes on her apartment in case someone came back and said he'd get to work immediately.

"Are you okay?" Tyler asked after disconnecting the call.

"I guess so. It's unnerving though."

He reached over and squeezed her hand. "I'm not going to let anyone get to you." And when he reassured her in that deep voice that set her nerves tingling, she believed him.

They drove in silence, his hand remaining possessively on hers. On the way, they passed the Meridian Hotel, owned by Tyler's father, Robert Dare. She wasn't surprised Tyler hadn't booked them a room there, given how he felt about his father. How all the Dare siblings felt. Although the girls tried hard to have a relationship with their father despite his failings, he'd hurt each one over and over again, until now none of them bothered.

And Ella didn't blame them. She, of all people, understood not having anything to do with a parent you'd once loved. There wasn't a day she didn't live with that knowledge and pain in her heart. But she was a better, healthier person for cutting ties and not wishing for something she could never have. And she was certain the same was true for Tyler and the rest of his family.

They arrived at the hotel, a white, unobtrusive stucco building on a corner that backed up to the beach. Tyler handed his car off to the valet, and her suitcase was whisked away by a bellman. They checked in, the lobby completely unconventional as far as Miami hotspots went. As soon as she stepped inside, Ella felt as though she were in a comfortable home. The taupe-and-white tones immediately put her at ease; there were books on the shelves and easy chairs for guests to sit in. The overall atmosphere was warm and inviting.

Next they were escorted to their room, and while Tyler tipped the bellman, Ella walked inside to explore. The king-size bed filled the room, surrounded by the serene tones of the white-and-sand furniture and accessories, which were made up of soft textures and pillows, a retreat that overlooked the ocean. It was a contrast of homey luxury.

Ella gravitated toward the sliding glass doors. She stepped out onto the balcony, and a warm breeze slid over her skin. She leaned on the railing and sighed with pleasure, listening to the rushing sounds of the ocean that both thrilled and relaxed her. With all the upheaval going on in her life, she was grateful for this chance to get away from the insanity she didn't understand. Who would be after her, and why? She didn't know. But she had Tyler to thank for bringing her here.

As if thinking his name conjured him, he joined her outside, stepping up behind her and winding his arms around her waist, pressing himself against her back.

"Like it?" he asked, nuzzling his mouth against her neck, causing her to shiver despite the warm air.

"It's beautiful here."

"You're beautiful," he said, sliding his lips along her skin.

She warmed at the easily spoken compliment. He seemed more at ease than he had before, and since she'd already decided to go with the flow as far as he was concerned, she gave herself over to the moment and turned in his arms. She tilted her head back in an open invitation, and he accepted, his mouth meeting hers.

The kiss was slow and easy, his tongue gliding against hers, lazily moving in and out, and ending with him nibbling on her lower lip. He nipped, and she moaned, arching her back, her body pressing not-so-subtly against his, meeting up with his hard, firm erection.

She inhaled his musky masculine scent, letting it work its way through her body and arouse her even more than his kiss already had. She leaned forward and kissed his jaw, sliding a hand up through his hair.

He caught her wrist, forcing her to meet his gaze. "I know I keep screwing things up, but I need you to know I'm going to try harder to get it right."

She didn't want promises he might not be able to keep. She knew where she stood with him, and she was okay with that. She had to be if she didn't want to get hurt.

"No talking," she said, freeing her hand. Bringing her fingers to the buttons on his shirt, she unfastened them one by one until she opened his shirt and pushed it off his broad shoulders.

She splayed her hands across his sculpted chest, feeling the play of hair-roughened skin and muscles beneath her fingertips. She lingered, his heart beating fast and furious beneath her touch, before leaning in and licking her way across his chest to his firm nipple. She pulled it into her mouth, teasing him with her tongue and teeth, until he groaned and his fingers bit into her skin.

He picked her up, and she wrapped her legs around his waist, and he backed them up, through the door, into the room, and tossed her onto the bed. Every time he took control this way, her heart raced harder and she fell more and more under his spell.

"I'm so fucking glad you prefer skirts," he said as he yanked said skirt down, taking her panties with it.

Moisture immediately pooled between her legs, her sex full and pulsing with need. Before she could react, he placed his hands on her thighs, pulled her legs apart, and leaned over her, his face inches from her wet heat. He stared down at her, a greedy look on his handsome face, and he parted her and slid his tongue over her weeping flesh.

She moaned, the sound causing him to delve deeper, licking, sucking, grazing his teeth over her nether lips until she was writhing on the bed. He was an expert at reading her body, knowing when to go soft, his tongue sliding gently around and over her clit, arousing her unbearably but not taking her over. Then he hardened his tongue and worked it inside her, greedily thrusting until she was pulling at his hair and begging for release.

Thank goodness he wasn't playing games. He added a finger to his repertoire, sliding it up inside her, her body

clenching at him, needing harder and more fulfillment than
he was giving.

"More, Tyler. Please, more."

He added a second finger and she groaned, arching
upward. His finger hit the right spot inside her, and she saw
stars behind her eyelids, screamed in a way that would have
embarrassed her had she been even minimally more aware.

He thrust in and out, each time hitting that spot until she
came hard, shuddering around him as he drew out her orgasm
until she lay weak and exhausted for a short time. She came
back to herself to find a gloriously naked Tyler leaning over her.

He brushed her hair off her cheek and grinned. "Sexiest
fucking thing I've ever seen."

She felt a flush rise to her cheeks. "Well, you did good.
Want a pat on the back?" she asked, grinning back.

"No, I want something more."

"Me too," she murmured, her exhaustion replaced by something else. Desire, heavy and thick, pulsed inside her once
more. She glanced down at his thickening cock and reached
out a hand, cupping him in her palm, feeling the smooth head
in contrast with all that hardness in her grip.

"Hands on the headboard," he ordered, and she had no
problem obeying his command. Especially since it meant he
was going to take her hard and satisfy the ache he'd had no
trouble creating.

He watched with glittering darkened eyes as she reached
up and grabbed on to the slats behind her. Biting down on her
lower lip, she drew a deep breath, mentally preparing herself
for what was to come seconds before he grasped her hips and
thrust home. That was the point when Ella realized she was
deluding herself if she really thought she could classify Tyler
Dare as just an affair.

Or as just anything. Because when he was inside of her like
this, he was her everything.

# Chapter Eight

*T*yler woke up around ten the next morning. He let Ella sleep in and headed downstairs to walk around the local shops and buy a bathing suit and pair of pool shoes, along with a shirt since he planned to take her to a nicer dinner later tonight. He hadn't planned on bringing her back to the hotel to have sex, since he'd meant what he said about spending time together in other ways, but he wasn't complaining about how easily they'd come together.

The sky was overcast, and it began to drizzle as he walked back to the hotel with breakfast for them both. They shared a comfortable morning, enjoying the muffins and coffee he'd brought back for them and talking about her job and how much she enjoyed the designing aspect and scoping out new ideas and trends. He shared how easily he'd fallen into security, choosing it because it was a natural transition from the army, and how he'd given his friends a soft place to land as well.

The only thing that marred a perfect morning was the trip to the police station for Ella to give and sign her statement for the cops. Once that was over, Tyler devoted himself to keeping her mind on more pleasurable things.

Holding hands, they spent the better part of the rainy day in the game room playing Ping-Pong with another couple who was also waiting for the sun to come out, which it finally did, late in the afternoon. And when they left to go shopping, Tyler and Ella played against each other.

It wasn't easy watching Ella dance around in denim shorts that showcased her long, tanned legs and allowed him to daydream about them wrapped around him while his cock was hard and buried in her feminine heat. She kept him from concentrating and displayed a competitive streak he enjoyed. Especially when she'd ace him at the table, lift her arms in the air, and dance around so her breasts bounced around beneath her cropped top.

They returned to the room and changed for dinner, Ella into a long white dress that fell off one shoulder, her hair in a messy bun. Before making their way to the restaurant he'd chosen, they walked on the sidewalk that ran parallel to the beach, taking their time, enjoying the view and each other.

"I didn't know you had that kind of competitive gene. I was impressed with your killer Ping-Pong skills," he said.

"There was a community center near my house, and I used to play. I won a game or two back in the day." She rubbed her knuckles against her chest and let out a laugh that echoed around them.

Damn but he liked hearing her relaxed and happy, and wished he could give her days like this more often. He'd called his team, and nobody had any answers so far about who could be behind the attempted break-in, so he didn't bring it up, not wanting reality to intrude on their night.

"I hope you like seafood. I made a reservation at a quiet place called The Rusty Pelican in Key Biscayne. It's about twenty minutes from here."

"Seafood works for me. I worked up quite an appetite beating you today." She met his gaze and winked, the small action so at ease he couldn't resist some more spontaneity.

He grabbed her around the waist, dipping her low. She squealed, and as he pulled her back up, he met her halfway, kissing her where they stood. He slid his lips over hers and devoured her mouth, hungry for her since last night.

They were interrupted by the sound of applause, and he held on to her, helping her keep her balance as she straightened. An older couple walking by had stopped and clapped before moving on.

He met her gaze as an adorable blush covered her cheeks.

"Come on. Let's go eat." He was looking forward to more time alone with her.

He drove to the restaurant, and a little while later, a hostess was leading them to the private table he'd requested in a secluded corner of the dimly lit restaurant. Unfortunately, it wasn't dark enough to hide another couple sitting close together in a round booth.

And just like when he was a kid, Tyler found himself facing his father in an obviously compromising position. They held hands on top of the table, not even bothering with discretion.

He wanted to keep walking. Hell, he wanted to run. After all, running was what he did best. But he realized this was a turning point for him, and instead of ducking away like he'd done something wrong, he straightened his shoulders and stopped walking, facing his father. In doing so, he pulled Ella to a halt as well. She came up beside him, and he felt, rather than saw, her stiffen. Obviously she was reading the situation at the table the same way he was. This wasn't a business meeting he'd intruded upon.

"Dad."

"Tyler." Even in the faint lighting, he couldn't mistake the ruddy flush staining his father's cheeks.

"You remember Ella Shaw?" Tyler placed a hand on her back, surprised his voice was steady.

Robert Dare nodded. He slid his napkin off his lap and pushed himself out of the booth, not introducing the woman beside him, who seemed to shrink into herself in the corner.

He stepped up to them.

"Maybe I should meet you at the table?" Ella offered, tilting her head toward the hostess, who was waiting patiently with the menus for them to continue along with her.

"No, you're with me."

Robert shrugged, as if to say, *suit yourself,* and Tyler pulled Ella tighter against him, drawing strength from her presence. The last time he'd been in this situation, he'd been young and alone. He appreciated knowing she stood by his side. It was a novel feeling, one he'd think about further when he'd put this mess behind him.

"This isn't what it looks like," his father said.

Tyler narrowed his gaze. "It's exactly what it looks like, just like it was when I was fourteen and walked in on you and Savannah."

Ella's sharp intake of breath reverberated around them, and Tyler hoped his old man squirmed.

"Okay then, if you insist on making this ugly, let's revisit what I told you then."

Tyler remembered every word.

*You don't want to be responsible for your mother's pain, son. Be a man. Keep my secret.*

"I don't owe Savannah anything," he said of his father's current wife, although he did have a relationship with his half siblings. "But whatever I decide to do about this? It'll be because I am a man who makes his own decisions."

Robert narrowed his gaze. "You wouldn't dare tell Savannah or the kids."

Tyler shrugged. "You don't know me well enough to know what I'd do, Dad. And whose fault is that?" he asked, not bothering to hide either his sarcasm or his disgust.

The man had done enough damage to Tyler's mother and siblings that it was a wonder any of them had moved on and were engaged in healthy, permanent relationships. Of course, they all had, except Tyler. And he was working on it.

"Come on, Ella." He nudged her into motion, leaving his father standing with his mouth open and hopefully with a very real fear in the pit of his stomach.

If he loved Savannah, he'd be in a full-blown panic. Although Tyler wondered if the man was capable of loving anyone but himself.

Before they walked away, Ella tugged at his hand. "Would you rather leave?" she asked.

He shook his head. "I'm finished letting him run my life in any way. We'll stay." He winked at her, intent on reassuring her he was okay.

Except, he realized as they walked away, his hands were shaking and his stomach was in knots, letting him know that, despite wanting to be fine, Robert Dare had once again shaken him to his core. The only difference was that this time, he wasn't about to let his father dictate how he'd deal with this newest revelation and betrayal.

Ella couldn't believe what she'd seen or how well Tyler had handled his father. He put up a good front, but she knew he had to be affected by what he'd witnessed and the confrontation they'd had—heck, she was too upset to eat.

And if he wasn't going to admit it, she was. "Tyler?"

"Yes?" He met her gaze, not bothering to hide the turmoil in his navy eyes.

She placed a comforting hand on his arm. "If you don't mind, I think I'd like to leave anyway. I've . . . I sort of lost my appetite," she murmured, giving him the out she sensed he needed.

He dropped his shoulders and groaned. "Can't say I blame you," he muttered. "Be right back." He walked over to the hostess and explained they wouldn't be staying, apologizing for holding her up and reserving a table they wouldn't be using.

They drove the trip back to the hotel in silence, Ella giving him the space she knew she'd need if the situation were reversed. Once they'd given the car to the valet, she turned to him.

"What do you say we go for gelato? There's a place we passed on the corner. We can skip dinner and go right for dessert. I'd say you could use it."

That got her a smile. "Why not?" Although he held her hand, he remained silent on the walk to the store.

She wanted him to open up, to know she'd be there for him the same way he was there for her, but she also knew he deserved privacy for the conversation. Coffee-flavored gelato for her and chocolate for him in hand, they walked back to the hotel. By the time they arrived, they'd each finished their dessert, and she was definitely indulging in a sugar rush from the treat.

"Want to head to the veranda?" she asked of the rooftop, which hosted a pool by day and a moonlit sky at night.

"Sure."

She waited until they were alone, settled together in a double swing chair in a private corner, before broaching the subject. As promised in the hotel brochures, the moon shone overhead, the stars twinkling in the inky night sky as they rocked back and forth. If the mood weren't so serious, she'd enjoy the scenery a lot more.

"You know you can talk to me. I won't repeat anything, and I won't judge."

He leaned forward and dipped his head, staring at his clenched hands. "It's complicated."

"Most families are." She nudged him with her knee. "Mine isn't exactly the poster child for stability, right? My dad's in prison, and we haven't spoken in years," she said, a lump forming in her throat. "Not to mention I spent vacations with your sister. I know what you all went through."

He kicked the ground, pushing the swing higher. "You don't know what I went through," he said, the pain in his voice as raw and tortured as his expression.

She grasped his hand. "Then tell me. You said something about walking in on your father and Savannah when you were fourteen?" she asked softly.

"I showed up at his office on a school holiday. I can't even remember why I went there now, but . . . yeah. I caught them . . . more in the act than what we saw tonight."

She winced at the image he presented, feeling sorry for the young boy who'd seen his father's failings at an age when he couldn't possibly understand.

"I take it he didn't act any guiltier than he did tonight?" She stared down at Tyler's big, tanned hand, running her thumb over his skin.

"No, he didn't feel bad at all. Savannah was horrified, but dear old Dad shifted the burden onto me." Tyler stiffened as he continued. "'You don't want to be responsible for your mother's pain, son. Be a man, keep my secret. It's better for everyone,'" he said in an imitation of Robert Dare.

And a damned good one too. Ella had never been comfortable around the man, but considering how little time he spent with his family, she hadn't had to see him all that often.

"You did what he asked?"

"I did." He met her gaze with his tortured one. "And it was a mistake. I should have told Ian or my mom. She could have found out in a way that cushioned the blow, instead of how my father chose to handle things." He ran a shaky hand through his hair. "'Hey, Emma, sorry to tell you like this, but I have another family and my youngest daughter has cancer, and I need your kids tested to see if their bone marrow matches,'" he spat out in disgust.

"I hope he told her more gently than that," she murmured. Though, seeing his callous behavior tonight, Ella doubted it.

"I wasn't there. I just remember the yelling, Mom's wailing and crying." His body trembled, and she wrapped an arm around him, resting her head on his shoulder. "It was the crying that was the worst. I'd hear her at night . . . and I thought if I'd just told her last year, maybe it would have been different or better. And I felt guilty because I had known."

"And you kept that inside? You never told your mom what you saw?"

He shook his head, eyes downcast.

"Ian? Scott?"

"Nope. My discovery, my betrayal, my fuckup. And that was just the beginning."

"Of what?" she asked, confused by whatever he was insinuating, but her gut told her he had so much twisted in his head, this ought to be a doozy.

He tipped his head back, resting on the striped cushions, staring at the starlit sky. "Of my pattern of running when things were emotionally difficult, of disappointing people," he said, the disgust in his tone catching her by surprise.

She blinked and immediately shook her head. "That's just not true."

Using his foot, he ground the swing to a sudden stop, rose, and began pacing in front of her. "You of all people can say that with a straight face?" he asked her.

"Tyler, I don't get it . . . what are you talking about?"

"I ran out on you the morning after. I was more of an adult than you were, and instead of staying to face what we'd done, I packed my things and headed right back to base. I know I blew it badly."

She sucked in a sharp breath, surprised he put her in the category of people he'd let down. "I thought we already agreed, I overstepped that night."

"And I handled it terribly. And it wasn't like I fixed things over the years either. I let things between us remain awkward and uncomfortable. We lied to my sister, and I treated you like shit." He ran a shaking hand through his hair, his emotions on the surface. "So yeah, that's all on me. Because I didn't face up to my responsibilities."

She doubted he'd be responsive to her arguments, so she remained silent, trying to find some way to reach him.

To her surprise, he continued. "I had a friend in the army. Serena's husband, Jack."

"Oh! I didn't realize you knew Serena before she came to work with you." Ella curled her legs beneath her, tucking her long dress discreetly around her.

This was the first time he was opening up and sharing with her, and despite the fact that he obviously blamed himself for things that didn't seem to be his fault, she treasured the insight and hoped she could help him through it.

"Serena and Jack were high school sweethearts. Jack was a happy-go-lucky guy . . . until the army and war got ahold of him. Then all he could talk about was getting out. And he did. Went AWOL and got himself killed. I don't want to discuss that tonight, but he's another example of a time when I should have done something. Could have prevented a tragedy from occurring."

Ella pushed off the swing and rose to her feet. "God," she said. "Excuse me?"

"That's who you must think you are, right?" Ella asked. "Because you really think you could control a lot of things. Like . . . your mom? She'd have been destroyed by the news no matter how she found out. And Jack? Even if you'd prevented him from leaving base, something inside him was clearly already broken." She drew a deep breath. "And as for me, I might have been legal, but I was just a kid. Even if you'd faced me the next day, it would have been awkward, and I'd have been mortified. I doubt much of how I viewed things would have changed." Her issues went deeper than her first sexual affair gone wrong.

Tyler's expression turned wry. "You're the second person who's told me I couldn't change things."

She walked over and took his face between her hands. "Then maybe you ought to listen?" she suggested, pulling him close for a lingering kiss.

He tasted of chocolate, and she couldn't help but moan as she licked at his lips, then slid her tongue inside, determined to make him forget about his troubles. And from the way he kissed her back, she'd quickly accomplished her goal.

He broke the kiss and said, "Come here."

Hands on her waist, he backed them up until he sat on the swing, pulling her down with him. She shifted until her knees were on either side of his thighs, her sex directly over the hard ridge of his cock through his jeans.

She rubbed against him and moaned as waves of pleasure ricocheted through her body. She grasped his shoulders and held on, just as he leaned forward and licked a path up her neck, nibbling on her earlobe. She trembled at his seductive licks and nips, and all the while, he worked her dress up around her waist.

"What about you?" she asked, bringing her hands to his fly and undoing the button.

"What about me?" he asked in a gruff voice.

"I want to touch you." She eased the zipper gently over his protruding erection, then slipped her hand into his briefs and freed his velvety shaft.

She slid her hand up and down, squeezing as she pumped, feeling his precum coat the palm of her hand. Desire pulsed through her veins, and her sex clenched with the need to have him inside her.

He let out a low growl and grabbed her wrist. "Hang on."

She slid her tongue over her lower lip. "I want you, Tyler. I want to feel you inside me."

His big hands cupped her breasts, kneading and plumping them through her top, until her nipples pebbled into tight peaks, and the aching between her thighs grew unbearable.

"And I want you to come around my cock," he rumbled in a gruff tone.

She trembled at his stark, honest words. "I want that too."

"Stand up."

She followed his command. Waited as he rose and pulled his jeans and boxer briefs down his legs, leaving them hidden by a table in front of the swing.

He sat back down, and she hiked her dress up, once again straddling him, but this time there was nothing between them except her panties. Nothing to stop the plump head of his cock from sliding through the damp folds of her sex, opening her to him as he thrust up and she took him completely inside.

She sucked in a startled breath at his width, allowing her body to get used to the feel of his heat, thickness, and length pulsing inside her. "God, you feel amazing."

"You feel pretty fucking spectacular too."

He surprised her by rustling the material of her dress, shifting the fabric around until their bodies were completely covered.

"Just in case we have company," he said with a sexy wink as he continued to shift and move inside her, every slight motion causing a ripple of arousal to take her that little bit higher.

But now that he'd mentioned it, she couldn't stop thinking about how they were outside and the possibility of being caught. To her surprise, the idea of someone walking in on them was mortifying . . . and oddly arousing.

She wrinkled her nose, wondering when she'd become this wanton woman willing to have sex in public. He was doing what he'd promised, soothing her old fears and insecurities, allowing her to become a butterfly emerging from her cocoon, braver and stronger than she'd been before. No matter what happened between them in the end, she'd owe him for showing her this side of herself, she thought.

"They'll still know," she whispered.

"But they won't *see*." He grinned. "How hot would it be if someone watched us like this?" He braced his hands on the bench and jerked his hips upward, the movement of the swing and the angle of his body hitting her in exactly the right spot.

"Oh!"

"Go ahead, sweet girl. Let me feel you come."

Her entire body shivered at his words, and she nearly flew apart when he continued to impale her with his shaft. Over and over, he thrust upward, and she met him each time, grinding her hips down, her clit hitting his pubic bone with each successive meeting of their bodies.

He took her hard and fast, and soon she was screaming, "Tyler, Tyler, Tyler!" as her world came apart, the stars she viewed brighter than the ones in the inky night sky.

He rammed himself upward once, twice, three times more. "Fuck!" He came, his hips jerking up and into her, causing aftershocks to rack her body until she collapsed against him, sweaty and spent.

He breathed heavily in her ear, his body lax against the cushions, the swing rocking beneath them. She'd clearly accomplished her goal, put his problems out of his mind, given him something else to focus on. And oh, had he focused on her, as he always did when they were intimately wrapped in each other.

He was inside her body, and she felt him there, and still, she wanted to get closer, to crawl into his skin. And that was the problem.

She was too wrapped up in him. Oh, she told herself she would protect her heart, but that same heart pounded hard in her chest, her emotions at the surface, too ready to break free. And that was something she couldn't allow because the risk of heartache was too great.

Tyler woke up in the hotel bed. He bolted upright, relying on senses that had served him well in the past, and knew immediately he was alone. Worried, he turned to Ella's side of the bed to find a note.

*Went to the lobby to get us coffee. Back in a few.*

She wasn't planning on leaving the hotel, and he breathed out a huge sigh of relief. No matter what went on between them, she was still in need of protection until they figured out who was targeting her and why.

He relaxed back against the pillows, his mind turning to last night. He couldn't believe he'd run into his father with another woman. Again. Not that he wished it on any of his brothers or sisters, but damn, he had the worst luck. And his father was a horrible human being. It was a miracle his siblings all took after their mother, because Robert Dare set the worst example as a parent that Tyler could imagine.

Before he could think on it and further ruin his morning, he heard the sound of the key card in the door, and Ella walked in, coffee tray in one hand and a bag in the other. She wore a pair of frayed denim shorts and a T-shirt that read *Bookworms Do It Better* across her lush breasts.

"Good morning. I have coffee and donuts," she said with a wide smile, her voice cheerful. "Jelly or powdered sugar?" she asked.

"I'll take option three: you. So put everything down and come here." He patted the side of the bed.

She placed the coffee and bag on the nightstand, kicked off her flip-flops, and joined him on the bed. "Are you upset about what you saw last night?" she asked.

"My father? I'm not thrilled, but you took the edge off," he said, pulling her into his arms.

"What are you going to do with the information?" she asked.

He breathed in the scent of floral shampoo in her soft hair, his dick rising to the occasion. "I'm not sure. I've gone over it in my head . . . My first instinct was to talk to Alex," he said of the half brother he was closest to of all his half siblings. "But then I realized I'd be putting him in the same position I was in when I was a kid."

She sighed and leaned her head against his chest. "Except he's an adult."

"Still not a burden I want to put on him."

She nodded against him. "I get that. What about talking to your mother? You mentioned yesterday feeling guilty about not telling her you knew about your father's affair earlier than the rest of the family. Maybe you could use last night as the impetus to open up to her. I'm sure she'll understand, and I know it'll help you feel better."

He leaned his head back and glanced at the ceiling. Her suggestion settled something that had always crowded his chest, causing him pain and guilt. Talking to his mom would probably ease a great burden and maybe even rid him of any uncertainties about his ability to make an emotional commitment.

"How did you get to be so smart?" he asked her.

"I don't know. Maybe because that's what I'd do if I were lucky enough to have my mom to go to," she said in a soft, wistful voice that made his heart clench and filled him with the desire to give her everything she was missing in her life.

And for the first time, he thought he was closer to being able to do just that.

# Chapter Nine

After a weekend that ended way too soon, Tyler took Ella home to her apartment so she could unpack and organize herself to come home with him for an indeterminate amount of time.

"I really would prefer to stay here at my place," Ella said, not for the first time since he'd informed her of his plan to keep her safe.

"And I'd prefer that whoever broke in didn't know where you live. We don't always get what we want."

She frowned at his gruff tone. Well, hell. What did she expect? After a weekend of intense intimacy, she was pulling away. He didn't blame her for not wanting to disrupt her life, but she didn't have to act so damned cavalier about leaving him.

She rubbed her arms and sighed. "Fine. I'll swap out my suitcase and pack up some things."

"Don't sound so thrilled about spending more time with me," he muttered.

"That's not how I mean it." She walked over, placing a hand on his waist. "I just don't want us to get too . . . comfortable with the situation."

"Us?" he asked, calling her out. "Or you?" Because for his part, he wasn't ready to drop her off here and leave her alone.

"Come on, Tyler. Neither one of us is in this for the long haul. You especially. Isn't this the longest you've been with any one woman? And let's face it, necessity is driving some of this togetherness."

He narrowed his gaze. "Really? After this weekend, that's how you want to play it?"

She exhaled a long breath. "I'm sorry. I am. I'm just on edge," she said, but he didn't believe that was the real reason.

She was uptight about them. And he needed to get his shit together completely so he could do something about it.

"I'll go pack," she said, and he let her go.

A little while later, she returned with two suitcases. "I have my laundry too," she said, placing the rolling bags near the front door.

"There's a pile of mail here," he reminded her. "Want to go through it before we go?"

She nodded. "Might as well. I usually catch up on the weekends, and I missed this one." She stopped by the table and sorted through her mail, tossing the garbage aside. "Oh, look! Wedding invitation." She looked on the back and smiled. "Your mom."

He smiled at that. "We all had our doubts when she met Michael, but he's been nothing but good to her. She deserves to be happy."

"That she does." She placed the invitation in her purse and looked through the last few items, freezing when she came to a plain white envelope, then dropping it to the floor as if it were poisoned.

"Ella?"

She didn't answer, so Tyler knelt down and retrieved the letter, glancing at the return address—a penitentiary in Florida.

"Oh shit." He rose and met her gaze. "When was the last time you heard from your father?"

"Not for almost ten years." She swallowed hard. "My aunt used to take me to see him because . . . well, he was my dad. But the visits were awkward, nobody spoke, and eventually we agreed going to the prison wasn't something either of us wanted."

"He hasn't written to you before?" he asked, because her reaction had been one of true surprise.

She shook her head. "It was like I was orphaned at fourteen," she whispered, breaking his heart. "What could he want now?" she asked.

He had no idea. He wrapped an arm around her, any lingering anger at her earlier withdrawal gone in a sudden burst of understanding. If she'd felt orphaned at fourteen, there was no way she had any basis of trust or faith in other people, he thought, a lump rising to his throat.

"Come on," he said, leading her toward the door. "We can talk about it over a drink at my place."

"Or maybe we can pretend I never received it in the first place," she muttered.

He'd let her get away with that for just so long. Long enough to process her feelings before he pushed her to resolve her childhood issues. She'd have to in order to have a future. And more and more, he was convinced he wanted that future to be with him.

Living with Tyler, Ella's emotions were all over the place, and now she had her father's letter to add to her worries. It was one thing to endure the knowledge that her father was in prison and they were estranged, another to hear from him, which brought up all sorts of painful memories and feelings of betrayal. Even at twenty-seven years old, she wasn't past the hurt.

She hadn't read the note, wasn't sure she wanted to. She tucked it away in her purse and tried to forget about it. She had other more pressing issues to deal with. Namely, her temporary change in address. Tyler lived in a house in Weston, not far from where his mother resided, one that he was renovating in his spare time, bringing in help when he needed it for bigger, more complicated jobs. He said he enjoyed the downtime and working with his hands. Considering she knew how talented he was with those hands, yeah. She figured he was putting his free time to good use.

He insisted she stay in his room, and since they were already sleeping together, she couldn't really argue. He drove her to and from work, wanting to be aware if someone was following her, and though she appreciated his diligence and caring, it was just another way she was getting too used to having him around. Making it even more difficult when things inevitably ended. In her world, good things usually did.

Yet for the next week, life fell into a normal routine. And Ella did well with routines. Routines had kept her centered as a child when she had little else to rely on. Life was normal. Or as normal as it could be with someone having tried to break into her apartment. Luke, it turned out, had taken a flight to St. Lucia to look into the mugging and break-in further. So on that count, Ella was in waiting mode.

With no other alternative, she pushed any negative thoughts out of her head and just lived. She did her job during the day, and at night she had dinner and amazing sex with Tyler. She'd never been in a relationship that clicked or worked, and there was a symmetry and sense of peace she was finding now. At the very least, she knew she was capable of more than she'd experienced before Tyler, giving her hope for her future. A future she refused to dwell on because . . . hello, she wasn't going to be negative and think about whether he would be in the picture even a week from now, after her situation was resolved.

The weekend rolled around and they decided to relax at home. Well, Ella relaxed while Tyler worked on the house. She couldn't say she minded the view, watching the substantial muscles in his back and arms flex as he moved. Although she claimed she was binge-watching a show, she'd admit to being distracted by the one he was unintentionally putting on. But when he started to use the sander, she nabbed his soundproof headphones and watched TV in another room.

She prepared him lunch, a pesto pasta salad with rotini pasta, tomato, and fresh mozzarella cheese, and he took a break to eat before getting back to work, thankfully not with the noisy sander.

She was finally relaxing and unwinding, just enjoying . . . life, when the doorbell rang.

"I've got it," she called. Tyler came up behind her, his warm body close to hers. "What are you doing? I can answer the door by myself."

"Just being safe."

She doubted anyone was going to come looking for her here, but she stepped aside and let him do his thing. He looked through the side window.

"It's Avery," he said, opening the door and letting her in.

"Hi, you two!" Avery said, joining them inside. She wore a pair of tight jeans and a loose, flowing Bohemian top in a mix of neutral colors and matching sandals.

"Hi!" Ella exclaimed, happy to see her friend.

"Just happen to be in the neighborhood?" Tyler asked, leaning against the side window.

"Good to see you too," Avery said, kissing her brother's cheek. "Actually, though, I was sort of in the neighborhood. I was visiting with Mom, and you're not far out of the way."

"Lucky me," he said with a wink. He liked to give her a hard time, but Tyler loved his sister, and Ella grinned, warmed by the relationship between the siblings.

"Well, good thing I'm not here to see you. I missed my best friend."

Ella tipped her head toward Avery. "Aww. Me too." She hugged her friend tight. "I hate having that empty room in the apartment, you know. We had a lot of fun."

"Something tells me you're having a lot of fun now." She wiggled her eyebrows.

"On that note, I'll leave you two alone," Tyler said, escaping from his sister's prying gaze.

Avery laughed aloud. "So," she said, turning to Ella. "*Are* you having fun?"

"You're a goof. And even if I wanted to tell you, neither one of us wants to discuss my *fun* with your brother."

"Eew." Avery wrinkled her nose and nodded. "Point taken."

"Come on in." Ella gestured for her friend to follow her to the kitchen. "Can I get you anything to eat or drink?" she asked, playing hostess . . . in Tyler's house, which felt odd.

"No thanks." Avery sat down at the smooth wood kitchen table and glanced around. "I realize this place is a work in progress, but you really need to spruce it up. It needs warmth. A woman's touch."

Ella rolled her eyes as she sat down beside Avery. "It's not my house."

Avery leaned in close, whispering, "Tyler's never brought a woman home with him before either."

"Well, maybe that's because no woman in his life has ever gotten herself into trouble before." Ella wasn't here because she was his girlfriend, and Avery knew all the updated details from their phone conversations. Ella was here so Tyler could make sure she was safe. Sex was a side benefit they'd both agreed upon earlier in their . . . relationship.

"I admit I was worried about that when we last spoke about you two being together, but he moved you in here. And when Grey moved me in with him, believe me, there was a hidden agenda. He wanted me with him and not just because of some stalker. So," she said, lowering her voice. "If my brother has you here, there's more to it than just safety." She nodded, as if she was wholly sure of herself.

But Ella couldn't afford to be so cavalier, because it was her heart on the line. Every night, when he thrust deep within her body and came without a condom inside her, she fell harder. She just refused to let herself acknowledge the words. The truth.

"Okay, change of subject. What else is going on with you?"

Ella glanced down, knowing she had to talk to someone about her father. Tyler had been gracious enough to give her space, but Avery had known her way back when. She'd been there for her when her life had been shattered by his selfish choices, so maybe she was the one to guide her now.

"I got a letter from my dad," she said.

"Oh, Ella. What did he say?"

She shrugged, embarrassed to admit the truth. "I haven't read it. I've been numb since it arrived. There were so many years when I wished he'd step up and be my father, and time after time, he disappointed me. I don't want to be hurt by him again."

Avery reached for her hand. "But you're hurting now, aren't you? Just thinking about the letter, you're hurting. So why not rip off the Band-Aid and see what's underneath?"

Ella exhaled a slow breath. "I'm scared."

"I know you are. And if you want me there when you read it, I will be. If you'd rather be alone, that's okay too."

"Thank you," she said over the lump in her throat. She knew she'd have to deal with the letter sooner rather than later. Just not right now.

They caught up about Avery's job, Grey's recording session, and other typical girl things. It was great to spend time with her best friend again. They were laughing over a joke Avery had read on Facebook when they were interrupted by the distinctive ring of Avery's cell phone.

Seconds later, Tyler's cell rang across the house. A concerned look crossed Avery's face, and she checked her phone. "It's my mom."

She answered her phone. "Mom, what's up?"

As she listened, the color drained from her face, and Ella rose, grabbing on to her for support. "I'm with Tyler and Ella. We'll all be right there."

She dropped the phone, and Ella disconnected the call for her. "What's wrong?"

"Olivia went into premature labor and something's wrong. We have to go now," she said at the same moment Tyler entered the room, his color as white as Avery's.

Ella rose, taking control. "Tyler, go put clean clothes on. We'll all go to the hospital together." She needed to be strong for them, even if she was as panicked and as frightened as they were.

Tyler paced the same room the family had shared while waiting for Scott and Meg's baby to be born. Unlike that happy occasion, today everyone was silent, trying not to panic. Only Meg and Scott were home with their newborn, sitting by the phone, waiting for a call.

Tyler didn't know much, just that Olivia had developed sudden and severe pain along with extremely heavy bleeding. Dylan had rushed her to the hospital, called Emma, and here they all were. They took turns pacing, sitting, worrying.

And all the while, Ella never left Tyler's side, for which he was grateful. She'd been a rock for both him and Avery from the minute their phones had rung.

"With this many people praying for her and the baby, everything has to be okay," he muttered when the silence surrounding him became too much.

Ella squeezed his hand. "I hope so."

Another hour had passed when Avery jumped up from her seat. "I have to go ask a nurse what's going on," she said, her voice shaking. "I can't just sit here and *wait*." She headed for the door, Grey right behind her.

"Can't say I blame her," Tyler muttered. He liked to think of himself as a man of action. Doing nothing while his sister was going through who knew what didn't sit right with him.

He rose to his feet just as Avery returned. "I found a nurse who promised to get someone to give us news soon."

Soon turned out to be another thirty minutes later, and Tyler counted every single one of them.

Finally, Dylan strode in, looking exhausted and wiped out. "Everything's okay," he said before anyone could jump on him with questions. "At least for now."

Emma walked over and pulled him in close. "How are *you?*" she asked.

"I'm holding up."

"What's going on?" Tyler asked.

Dylan ran a hand over his goatee. "Olivia was nauseous, so I had her lie down, then she started having what she thought were contractions, and then she began hemorrhaging. I rushed her here. They did a nonstress test and an ultrasound. The baby looks okay, but they're not sure what's going on." He exhaled a tired breath. "The important thing now is to try and hold off labor. At the very least, they'd like to get her to thirty-seven weeks, and we're at thirty-six. If the contractions continue, though, we're having a baby tonight."

Dylan glanced around the room, his gaze taking in the entire family. "I'm really grateful you're all here, but I think you can go home and wait for a call. If they stop the contractions, there's no baby tonight, but we could still be here for the duration. At least until she's stable."

"Thank you, Dylan." Emma kissed him on the cheek. "Go back to my daughter and tell her I'm with her in spirit."

"Thank you," he said in a gruff voice. He inclined his head and walked out.

"I'm not leaving," Emma immediately said, her voice cracking with emotion.

Michael, her fiancé, a man Tyler and all his siblings had come to respect, took her hand. "You need to rest. If Olivia needs you, what good will you be to her if you're too exhausted to stand?"

"He's right," Ian added. "I'm taking Riley home too. Rainey's got a cold, and we want to check on her."

"I'll stay," Tyler said, knowing he wouldn't stop worrying just because he went home.

"I'll stay with you," Ella said, her tone indicating she wasn't going to let him argue.

She'd be surprised to know he hadn't planned on arguing. Not only did he not want to be alone, he wanted her by his side.

"Okay, then you call me no matter what time of night it is," his mother said. "Good news, bad news, I want to be the first to know."

"I promise," Tyler told her.

As everyone gathered their things, the door to the waiting room opened once more.

Tyler glanced up, shocked to see his father walk in. Wearing his usual suit and tie, immaculately dressed, and not a hair out of place, he strode in like he owned the place.

Tyler made his way across the room in a heartbeat. "What are you doing here?" he asked, blocking his father from coming any closer.

He felt, rather than saw, Ian flank him on his left side. And though he appreciated his brother's support, Tyler wanted, no, he needed to handle this on his own. After what he'd witnessed the other night and the way his father had treated him over the years, standing up for his sister, for his family, felt personal.

Robert narrowed his gaze. "My daughter's here."

Tyler ground his molars together in anger and frustration. The man's gall knew no bounds. Each sibling had a reason for having pulled further and further away from their father in recent years, and no one wanted him around in a time of crisis.

"Who told you Olivia is here?" Ian asked.

"Excuse me?" Robert straightened his shoulders, his defenses up.

"Who told you Olivia is here?" Tyler repeated Ian's question.

Because he knew for damned sure no one in this room had made that phone call. Robert Dare was the last thing his stressed-out family needed.

"Stuart Jameson called me."

"A hospital trustee," Ian muttered.

Robert rolled his shoulders back. "Word travels fast when a major benefactor of the hospital has a relative admitted," he said in an arrogant tone. "However, one of you should have informed me."

"Why?" Tyler asked.

"Because I'm her father. I'm *your* father," he said angrily.

"When it's convenient," Tyler spat. "Like when you needed bone marrow. Or you need to guilt one of us into doing your bidding." He stepped closer and whispered so only his father heard, "Or you need us to keep your sordid secrets."

"That's uncalled for." Robert raised his voice, causing Ian to place a hand on Tyler's shoulder in a show of solidarity.

"I'm calling it like I see it, *Dad*. Without running down your sins against each of us individually, let's focus on what's important. Olivia is fighting to hold on to her baby. Olivia, whose last birthday party you didn't bother showing up for. You couldn't even be bothered to call. So if you're here now, there's a reason. One that benefits only you."

"Tyler!" his mother said in a concerned voice from behind him.

She didn't stand up for Robert, but she always expected her children to be civil. She couldn't possibly understand why he was turning on his father now, after all this time.

Tyler shook his head, not wanting her to interrupt him until Robert was gone. Later, when Olivia and her baby were out of the woods, he'd explain why he was taking this stand now.

"I've got this, Mom. We'll talk later," he said without looking back at her, never tearing his gaze from his father's angry one.

"You're wrong," Robert said stiffly.

"I doubt it." Tyler paused in thought.

What reason could Robert be here, caring about Olivia's welfare? Because Stuart Jameson knew Olivia was here. He'd check on her. And he'd hear if the great Robert Dare had been by. Or someone could tip off the media and Robert would need to be seen here. Those were the only scenarios that made sense.

Tyler glared at his old man. "I'm going to assume you're here because you're afraid someone on the board will find out you're not the family man you claim to be. Or worse, the press gets wind of the fact that you're a fraud. Well, newsflash, Dad: You aren't wanted or needed here."

His father's complexion turned a ruddy color. "You're being disrespectful and rude."

"He's just telling the truth," Ian said. "Something we all should have done years ago instead of trying to give you chance after chance because the girls have soft hearts."

Sweat broke out on the older man's forehead, but Tyler couldn't bring himself to feel sorry for his father. He couldn't bring himself to feel anything beyond disgust.

"Just go home," he muttered.

And when no one else in the room disagreed with him, Robert let out a loud huff, turned, and strode out, slamming the door behind him.

Tyler released the breath he hadn't been aware of holding. Ignoring Ian's curious gaze, he spun toward Ella, who pulled him into her warm embrace.

She rose on her tiptoes. "I could kiss you right now," she whispered.

His mouth twisted in a wry grin. "Are you telling me that seeing me tell him off was a turn-on?"

She burst out laughing, breaking the tension his father's presence had caused.

"Tyler, what was that all about?" his mother asked, pulling his attention away from Ella and back to the unpleasantness that was Robert Dare. "I know there's often no love lost, but none of you has ever been so outright . . . mean to him. At least, not recently."

She was right. Over the years, after the initial hurt and anger, they'd made peace as best they could. He exhaled a harsh breath and headed to his mother.

He grasped her cold hands in his. "Look, I promise to tell you everything when the time is right. But tonight, can we just focus on Olivia? She needs our prayers, and that's all I want to deal with right now."

Emma eyed him with her sternest mom glare. "Tyler, you try my patience. You always have. But yes, I want to focus on Olivia too." She patted his cheek. "Don't think I'm going to forget or let you blow me off though."

"I wouldn't dream of it," he said, grateful for the reprieve.

Because worrying about Olivia was taking all of his strength—what was left anyway, after that confrontation. But for the first time since walking in on his father with his mistress, Tyler felt . . . empowered. Not burdened by Robert Dare's expectations or secrets. He was his own man at last.

# Chapter Ten

*E*lla woke up on the hospital waiting room couch, stretched out beside Tyler. Every muscle in her body ached from the uncomfortable sofa and the unnatural position in which they'd slept. She wondered what had woken her, then she heard the distinctive sound of throat clearing. She opened her eyes to Dylan holding out a cigar for Tyler, a big grin on his weary face.

Tyler pushed himself to sit, and Ella followed, easing herself into an upright position, stretching as she moved.

"It's a girl," Dylan said. "And mother and baby are doing fine."

"That's great news!" Tyler said, the relief in his voice unmistakable. It had been a long night of worrying and very little sleep.

"Congratulations!" she said to Dylan. Two babies in this family in such a short amount of time. So much joy, she thought, happy for them.

"Thanks. They've got the baby in the NICU, but her lungs are formed, and everything else looks good," he said, sounding thankful. "Considering she's early, I am so damned relieved."

Tyler nodded in agreement, the taut muscles in his face gone in favor of a huge smile. "I'll call the rest of the family."

"Or at least get the phone chain started," Dylan said with a laugh. "Ask everyone but Emma to hold off visiting until tonight, okay? Olivia is wiped out and slightly anemic from loss of blood."

"I will. I'm so fucking relieved and happy for you." Tyler extended his hand for Dylan to shake. "Give my sister a kiss for me."

Dylan grinned. "Will do. I can't thank you enough for staying the night, but you two should go home and get some sleep."

Tyler rose, helping Ella to her feet. "Can't argue with that idea." He patted Dylan on the back before the other man left, heading back to his wife.

Tyler, looking adorably disheveled in a pair of jeans and an old T-shirt he'd changed into before they left for the hospital yesterday, turned to Ella.

She'd changed too, but she had a hunch adorable wasn't a word she'd use to describe what she looked like that morning.

"What do you say we get some breakfast before heading home?" he asked.

The word *home* took her off guard. His house wasn't her home. Her stomach chose that moment to grumble, loudly. "Umm, sure. Breakfast sounds good," she said, grateful for the distraction.

"Okay, let me make a few phone calls, and we're good to go."

After the family had been notified, they headed over to a Waffle House near the hospital. Starving, Ella shamelessly ordered a stack of chocolate chip pancakes, bacon, and a steaming cup of coffee, hoping to jump-start herself for the day.

Their orders arrived quickly, and Ella didn't hesitate or take time for small talk. She dug into the delicious-smelling meal and didn't come up for air until she heard Tyler laughing.

She glanced at him over her coffee cup, then slowly lowered it to the table. "What?" she asked.

"A girl after my own heart. I love your appetite."

Her cheeks burned hot. "We missed dinner," she muttered.

"I know." He waved his hand over his empty plate, his Spanish omelet, home fries, and fruit all gone too. "I was just enjoying watching you." He studied her with amusement in his navy eyes.

"Well, it was good. And now I'm full." Because there was nothing left on her plate, not that she'd admit as much.

"Then my mission is accomplished." He winked at her and took a sip of his coffee.

She sighed. "Well, the one good thing about that meal is that I got my second wind."

"Me too. Did you want to go home and get lucky?" he asked, those sexy eyes staring into hers.

She wished that was what she had in mind. "Much as I'd love to, I had something much more serious I wanted to talk to you about."

He raised an eyebrow. "Something wrong?"

She swallowed hard. Ever since watching him take on his father on behalf of his sister and the rest of the family, her mind hadn't stopped spinning with thoughts of her dad and her own family. Or lack thereof.

"Last night, when you confronted Robert Dare, I was—"

"Turned on by my inner alpha?"

She shook her head and laughed. "Yes to that. But I was also inspired by the closeness you share with your family and the passionate way you stood up for yourself at last."

He leaned in close. "Not that I'm not flattered, but I sense you have a bigger point to make than complimenting me?"

She shrugged. "Caught me. Actually you got me thinking about all the unresolved issues in my own life."

He reached across the table and clasped her hand in his bigger warm one. "You're talking about the letter from your father, aren't you?"

She nodded.

"Have you read it?"

"No." She curled her hand around his, drawing strength from his support, his presence, his touch. "I've been afraid."

"I'm proud of you, and I'm here for you, whatever you need," he promised.

She smiled at that. "Thank you. It's already because of you that I'm ready to read it. You gave me courage."

"I'll give you a lot more than that if you give me the chance," he said in a low, husky rumble.

She squirmed in her seat at his sex-infused tone of voice. Suddenly, she wanted nothing more than to head home and climb into bed with Tyler, making the most of whatever time they had together. She meant what she'd said. She absolutely intended to deal with her father's letter. After she let Tyler have his way with her.

Tyler lived up to his promise at the Waffle House, bringing Ella home and making sure she was well pleasured. They spent the day alternating making love and napping because they'd had very little sleep the night before. Dinner consisted of take-out pizza and binge-watching TV before they crashed early, knowing they had work the next day.

As he dropped her off at work, leaning across the car for a prolonged kiss, he realized how his life had changed in a short time. And how much he was grateful for the shift.

He'd never thought he'd become domesticated, despite having bought a house. A part of him had thought he might finish the place and flip it, making money on the resale. But now, having had Ella there for the last week or so, he liked the routine they'd fallen into. He loved knowing he'd see her at the end of every day, listening to her animated stories of her workday on the ride home. He even enjoyed the bickering over what to eat for dinner, who'd cook and who would clean, and what to watch on TV.

He knew his feelings for her were deep, and growing every day. And when she'd curled up with him on the hospital couch, staying with him when she could have caught a ride home with Avery and Grey, he acknowledged what he'd already known deep down inside.

He was in love with her.

She was everything he'd never known he wanted or needed in his life. Someone who put up with his shit, who understood his past and hang-ups and current needs. She stuck by him during tough times, as the last weekend and last night had proved. Now he needed to do the same for her or when this mess with her being followed was over, he'd lose her for good.

According to Luke, he was onto something with her boss and was digging deeper. Tyler wasn't surprised considering everything had started in St. Lucia. But he didn't want to share the information with Ella just yet. She wouldn't be comfortable at work, and his gut told him the boss herself wasn't the direct issue. Something else was going on. And until Luke figured it all out, Tyler intended to use his time with Ella to his advantage.

But right now, he had to head over to his mother's. She'd visited with Olivia and her new granddaughter that morning, something Ella and Tyler planned to do after work. He was meeting up with his mom at her house that afternoon.

He found her in the kitchen, an explosion of pots and pans around her.

"Testing recipes for an upcoming cooking class," she explained, wiping her hand on her apron and rushing over to greet him. His mother had begun teaching cooking classes out of the house, feeding a passion she'd always had. They'd eaten well growing up, he recalled fondly.

His mother hugged him, and he grinned at the mixed scent of cinnamon and the perfume he always associated with his mother, a warm, familiar smell that reminded him of home. He squeezed her tight. "Hi, Grandma."

She laughed with delight. "That never gets old. Did you hear? They named the baby Annie," she said, smiling wide.

"I heard. Ella and I are going over to visit tonight."

"That's good. Now let's talk," she said, getting right to the point of this visit. "Because what I witnessed last night was very unlike you."

"How about I sit down?"

She waved him toward the barstools near where she was working, and he settled in.

"That bad?" his mother asked. She untied her apron and smoothed the wrinkles in her taupe slacks and white blouse. His mother was always dressed well, no matter what she chose to do.

He shrugged. "Well . . . yeah."

"Why don't you start at the beginning," she suggested, sitting down beside him.

"Okay. I went to a small out-of-the-way restaurant last weekend, and I ran into Dad."

"He was out with Savannah?" his mother asked.

Over the years, they'd all come to terms with the facts of their lives. Robert had remarried and moved on. And finally, Tyler's mother was doing the same.

His mother didn't seem to hold a grudge . . . no more than she had to, anyway. Tyler always assumed that was what had allowed her to move on with another relationship, letting go of that part of her past. Children not included, of course. Nobody was more important to Emma than her kids.

"Actually, he was with another woman."

His mother's head shot up, her eyes wide. "Business associate?"

He shook his head. "Definitely not. And Mom, look. It wasn't the first time I walked in on Dad in a compromising position." His stomach cramped at the admission he'd been holding in for so long.

His mother tucked her hair behind one ear and narrowed her gaze. "What do you mean?"

He swallowed hard. Now that the moment was here, he was nauseous and unsure he could go through with the telling. "You know what? It's not important."

He rose to his feet, but his mother grasped his hand. "Sit back down and talk to me."

He lowered himself back into the chair, drew a deep breath, and just spit it out. "When I was fourteen, I walked in on Dad and Savannah . . . you know. At his office."

"That bastard!" She slammed her hand against the granite, catching her mistake immediately as she grabbed her hurt fist.

"Are you okay?" Concerned, he lifted her hand, checked it over where she'd made contact.

"I'm fine. I'm just annoyed with that selfish SOB for putting you in that position. Anyone could have walked in on him, and I can't believe it was one of his children." She met his gaze with her own somber one.

"Mom, I don't think you've done the math. It was a full year before we found out about his other family." He paused to let his words sink in.

"Oh, Tyler. Why didn't you ever say anything?" she asked, her hand over his.

"I was weak and it was wrong. I could have spared you hearing about it in Dad's callous, demanding way." His heart squeezed tight in his chest, guilt and loathing filling him, even as he hoped his mother could forgive him.

"What? No! That's not at all what I'm saying. You're my baby boy. I can't believe you lived with that knowledge all this time. Did you tell your brothers? Share the burden with someone?" she asked.

He tipped his head, unsure he'd heard her correctly. "You're worried about me?"

She touched his cheek in that motherly way of hers. "Of course I am. That's not something any child should see, let alone have to keep inside."

He leaned against the counter, taking comfort from the cold granite through his shirt. "That's not what Dad said."

She narrowed her gaze. "He saw you? He knew you caught him? I just assumed you caught a glimpse and ran out. What did he tell you?"

"To shut my mouth so I wouldn't hurt my mother. To be a man and keep his secret." His throat hurt as he repeated the words that had haunted him for over a decade. "So I did."

"Oh, honey." His mother pulled him into her arms. "You're a good, decent man. I'm sorry you had to live with that all these years and revisit it again now."

"Thank you," he said, his head still spinning from the unexpected way this conversation had gone.

True, Ella thought his mother would have been devastated no matter when she'd learned of her husband's betrayal, but Tyler had never factored her worry or concern for *him* into her reaction.

"You're special, Mom. I think that's why we all turned out okay." He stepped back and seated himself again.

She smiled at him in gratitude. "So that's why you threw him out of the waiting room."

"We should have done it years ago. Every year he's hurt one of us more and more. Olivia was devastated when he didn't show up for her birthday party. Why would she want him there? Why would any of us?"

On that subject, his mother remained silent, choosing discretion over bashing Robert Dare further.

"So what are you going to do with this information now?" she asked him.

He shook his head at the question that had plagued him, but he'd already come to a decision. "Initially I didn't plan on doing or saying anything. I couldn't see burdening them with this. But after last night, I think there will be questions. I'm going to have to tell them."

She nodded. "They're curious," she agreed.

"But my half siblings?" He shrugged. "It's not my place, and they don't need to live with it the way I did. Unless Olivia or Avery feels like they need to tell them. They're close." He ran a hand over his eyes. "I wish he hadn't shown up last night. I could have kept it to myself."

"Maybe that was a sign you're not meant to be alone in all things," his mother mused. "Ever think of that? You have a family you can share things with."

"You're right. I'm just coming to appreciate everyone even more now." Seeing how alone Ella was, how could he not be more thankful for his own family support and unconditional love?

Emma cleared her throat. "What about Savannah?" she asked.

He shook his head. "Wish I knew. I guess that'll play out if her kids find out. And to be honest . . . if you get someone by cheating, can you really expect anything different?"

"No," she murmured.

"All I know is that this time, I can live with things a lot better, knowing I'm making my own decisions. Not ones Dad demands."

"You're thinking for yourself. Like the strong, intelligent man you are." She touched his cheek. "Don't lose sleep over your father, honey." She shrugged. "I'm really not sure what else to say."

"I think you've said it all. You straightened my head out after so many years. I just can't believe I kept it to myself all this time."

"So . . . what about you and Ella?" his mother asked, changing the subject abruptly. Clearly she was finished with Robert Dare.

"In the beginning, the issues were my own." Or at least that was what he'd thought.

"What do you mean?" she asked, studying him with the concerned gaze of a loving parent, reminding him how lucky he was to have had her to counteract his callous father.

He rested his arms on the cool countertop. "Well, for years, I felt like I ran out instead of facing emotionally tough decisions. Case in point, not telling you about Dad and Savannah."

"For God's sake, you were all of fourteen!"

"How about joining the army to get away from him? Instead of sticking by my family and being here for you all?"

She shook her head, her lips drawn into a firm line. "Tyler Dare, at eighteen, I don't think anyone makes truly perfect, rational decisions. And if you joined the army for those reasons, then you needed to get away, and you deserved to live your own life. Make your own choices and mistakes. What else are you carrying around like a ten-ton weight?"

He decided to keep that night with Ella to himself. The same with Jack going AWOL. He already understood the pattern he'd weighted himself with wasn't an accurate one. He hadn't run, he'd made choices that were the only ones he could make at the time.

"Nothing. I understand things better now." He understood himself better. "I was worried I couldn't commit to Ella . . . or any woman because of my past choices. But I see now that wasn't the right way to view things."

"You're sure?" his mother asked. "Because we can sit here all day until you understand that you're only responsible for yourself and your decisions. And none of the ones you've made have been so awful."

He grinned at her, knowing she was right.

"Good, because it's life. We live and we learn." She rose and kissed his cheek. "What about Ella? Does she understand that?"

Tyler groaned. "I wish she did, but she has more to work out." He paused, then decided to confide in his mother. "She received a letter from her father in prison. Apparently they've been estranged for years. I want to help her get past it, but she has to be ready."

Emma nodded. "Knowing she has you has to make things easier. The poor girl's been alone for too long."

If Tyler had his way, she wouldn't ever be alone again. But Ella had a lot of practice doing things on her own, and that made him nervous. It had him wondering if she'd even be capable of truly opening up her heart.

"Thanks for understanding, Mom. Thanks for everything." He kissed her cheek.

"Always." Emma smiled, back to the bright, happy expression she'd had when talking about her grandbabies. "Now I need to get back to this baking or I won't be ready for tomorrow's class. Do you want to stick around? I'll let you eat the scones when I'm finished."

He laughed. "I'll take a rain check." He had a woman to pick up from work, and they had important things to discuss.

While visiting Olivia and her baby, Ella experienced an unexpected jolt of longing, similar to the one she'd felt while watching Tyler hold Mcg's baby boy. Considering how much she had going on in her life aside from Tyler—someone trying to break into her apartment and her estranged father rearing his head—she didn't need any more emotional upheaval on her plate.

But living with Tyler, going through the motions as if they were a couple with a future, how could she not feel a need for more in her life than she'd have without him? Yet, unless and until she straightened her head out, she couldn't begin to think about anything beyond the here and now.

By the time they returned to his place, she was exhausted and in need of alone time, where she could get her head back on straight. She excused herself, and Tyler said he'd let her know when dinner was ready. She didn't know what he was preparing, and she didn't much care. She was just grateful she didn't have to cook it tonight.

With her head pounding, she headed for her bag, looking for some ibuprofen that she kept on hand. Frustrated when she couldn't find the small bottle, she dumped the contents of her bag onto the bed . . . and the letter from her father fell out.

She picked up the envelope, now dirty and worn from traveling in her purse, and settled onto the bed. She'd told herself she needed to read the contents, and she took this as a sign it was time, whether she was ready or not.

She stuck her nail under the flap and opened the envelope, pulling out the paper and unfolding it. Two pieces of paper fell out: a visitor's application and a handwritten letter. Drawing a deep breath, she began to read.

Dear Ella, I know it's been a while. Far too long, really . . .

She recognized her father's handwriting, the scratchy penmanship causing a lump to form in her throat. There'd been a time after her mother had died when he would help her with her homework, making notes for her to look at later in the same nearly illegible hand.

She swallowed hard and noticed at a glance that the note wasn't long.

You may not believe me, and I don't blame you, but I miss you and think of you every day. I understand why you no longer come visit, and I even believe that I wouldn't deserve it if you did. For that reason, I'm going to come right out and tell you what you need to know, without me sugarcoating the words. I'm dying.

A sob rose up in her chest, bursting forth from her throat. Feelings she hadn't known she had, and would have denied if asked, bubbled forth, and she began to rock back and forth on the bed, tears dripping down her face as she continued to read on.

The doctors said I have end-stage lung cancer. Guess all those cigarettes I smoked along with the booze finally caught up with me. Though I have no right to ask, and was never there for you when you needed me, I'd like to see you one last time. If nothing else, I'd like to apologize in person and to tell you I love you the same way. You need to fill out the application and return it if you decide to come. Yours, Dad.

Ella wiped her cheeks with her palms, but the tears kept flowing, with big hiccupping sobs she couldn't control.

"Ella, dinner!" Tyler called, obviously thinking she'd showered already.

She glanced around his bedroom, the large king-size bed and the two nightstands and matching wooden furniture around the room. Though she wasn't alone in the true sense of the word, not while she was in Tyler's house and surrounded by him in all ways, she'd never felt more isolated and abandoned.

*Tell him,* a voice in her head said. *Tell him and he'll hold you and make it all better.*

"It's temporary," she replied, as if it made sense to talk out loud. And if there was one thing she knew how to do, had had to learn how to do, it was to survive on her own.

"Ella?" he called up to her again.

"I'm not hungry," she yelled back. Leaving everything on the bed, she grabbed an oversized shirt of Tyler's and a pair of her underwear before closing herself in the bathroom and turning the shower on full steam. She stripped off her clothing and shut herself in the glass enclosure, letting the burning water rush over her skin.

While there, she cried hard, unleashing the emotions rampaging through her at the thought of losing another parent. Because, she realized, although they hadn't had contact, it meant something to know her father *lived* somewhere in this world. The fact that he soon wouldn't meant she'd wasted so much time and energy on being hurt and angry. She'd spent all this time without him when maybe they could have healed their rift. And she was the one to blame, because really, how could he have visited her from prison?

*He could have written before now*, that voice reminded her. But she wasn't listening, not when it felt like the weight of the world sat on her shoulders and every decision she'd made had been the wrong one. So she cried some more, for the mother she'd lost and who hadn't seen her grow up, for the father who'd all but thrown her away, and for not trying once more with him before it was too late.

She'd go see him, she decided, but when all was said and done, he'd be gone from her life for good. And she'd be left as alone as when she'd started.

# Chapter Eleven

yler heard Ella answer his call for dinner, a mumbled sound he couldn't understand. He gave her some time before heading up to see what was keeping her. He walked into the room to find her pocketbook on the comforter, contents spread all over. The shower ran in the bathroom. He scooped up the tissues, wallet, and other things, tossing them back into the leather purse, and then he came to the handwritten letter and visitor's application left open on the bed. He picked those up too, intending to fold them up and put them away, but he couldn't help notice the tear stains on the paper, smudging the ink.

And though it was wrong, and rude, he scanned through the document anyway, muttering a low, succinct curse when he got to the end.

"That stupid, selfish bastard."

So he wanted to see his daughter, but couldn't he have told her the news in person instead of dumping it on her that way? There were so many other ways this could and should have gone down, but then every choice Harry Shaw had made in life had been the wrong, most hurtful one. At least when it came to his only daughter.

Leaving the letter on the nightstand, he headed for the bathroom, stripping his clothes off as he walked, intending to join Ella in the shower and care for her the way she needed.

Except when he reached the bathroom and pushed the door open a fraction, a loud sob reached his ears, breaking his heart.

He joined her in the steamy shower, shutting the door behind him and pulling her into his arms. Trembling, she plastered herself against him and let go, her tears mixing with the water sluicing down his chest.

"Let it all out," he said, stroking her hair with one hand, holding her upright with the other.

He wouldn't have thought it possible, but she cried harder, her body quaking and trembling, the sounds coming from inside her, raw and painful to hear.

It took what felt like forever, until finally her sobs quieted down just as the water began to cool. "Are you okay?" he asked.

She stepped out of his embrace and nodded, wiping her eyes with her hand as he shut off the faucet, freeing them from the now too-cold water.

"You didn't have to come in," she said, reaching for the towel.

He took it from her and gently wrapped the bath sheet around her body. "Of course I did."

She sniffed and met his gaze, her makeup streaked beneath her eyes. "Thank you. But I just needed a few minutes alone and—"

"The last thing you need is to be alone." He grabbed his own towel from the hook behind the door and quickly dried himself off before tucking the towel around his waist.

"You saw the letter."

It wasn't a question, so he merely nodded. No point in denying it. She'd left it out on the bed. "I'm so damned sorry."

She raised a delicate shoulder, then lowered it again. "It shouldn't matter, right? He hasn't been in my life for years."

"Actually, it matters a hell of a lot." He stepped forward and brushed the black streaks off her cheek with his thumbs, then wiped the stains onto the towel. "If Robert Dare died next year, do you think I'd be able to go on as if nothing happened? That it wouldn't affect me? That I wouldn't grieve?"

"I know, but doesn't it make me a hypocrite to care now?"

"It makes you soft, warm, and human." He looked into her beautiful hazel eyes. "It's just one of the reasons I love you," he said, the words escaping without permission. At the worst possible time.

Her lips parted in a soft *oh*. "Tyler," she breathed in a low voice. The same husky voice she used crying out his name when he was buried deep inside her wet, willing body.

He placed a hand over her parted lips. "Do not say another word. And sure as hell don't answer me now. I don't want to hear anything you have to say while you're an emotional wreck."

"But—"

He braced his hands on her cheeks, slowly stroking her soft skin. "Just live with it awhile and know that no matter what you believe, you aren't alone."

"Not now I'm not," she murmured, raising herself up on tiptoes to kiss him on the mouth, parting her lips immediately, seeking entry.

He understood she needed to forget her troubles, and he wanted to give her the peace she sought, so without another word, he swept her into his arms and carried her out of the bathroom and over to the bed. Laying her down on the mattress, he pulled the sides of the towel open and unwrapped her, revealing her ripe, perfect breasts, sweet, puckered nipples, and flat stomach. His gaze traveled lower, over her belly button and the smooth skin beneath, trailing down to the neatly trimmed thatch of hair covering her sex.

Keeping her distracted was key, so he zeroed in on his target and cupped his hand over her mound, sliding one finger around her slippery folds. Back and forth, he coated her in her own juices, torturing her as she writhed against his hand. Tormenting himself. His cock didn't appreciate being ignored, especially when he was hard and painfully erect, but this wasn't about him right now.

"Mmm. Tyler," she moaned, arching her hips against his hand and rocking against him, seeking relief.

"I like to hear my name in that sexy voice."

She reached out and clasped his erection in one hand, pumping up and down his straining shaft until liquid pooled at the top. "I want to taste you," she whispered, gripping him tighter, sliding her hand up and down, tightening when she hit the base, loosening as she slipped upward, then gripping him harder again at the head.

"Fuck," he muttered, his eyes rolling back.

"That's the idea," she said, a sexy grin lifting her lips.

Under any other circumstances, he'd agree. But he'd told her he loved her, and there was no way he was going to fuck her hard now, as if she didn't matter to him. No way he would let her screw him *just* to forget her problems.

A side benefit? He was all for that. But never again would he take her without showing her how much he cared at the same time.

Unfortunately, she was on a mission, not thinking about emotions, only looking to feel good and forget. As a guy who used to react the same way, he didn't miss the irony that now he wanted something more, deeper and more meaningful.

She pushed at his shoulders, and he rolled onto his back, easing himself up farther on the bed. With a determined glint in her eyes, she set one knee on either side of his legs and straddled him, lowering herself until her mouth was inches away from his rock-hard cock.

She deliberately breathed out, her warm breath wrapping him in teasing heat, and he curled his hands into the comforter, attempting to focus on anything but the blood pumping through his veins and settling in his dick.

Before he could prepare himself, her tongue snaked out, and she licked the precum off the head, causing electricity to shoot through his body. He bucked up, his cock jutting straight out, and she caught him between her waiting lips. Once her warm breath and slick tongue got hold of him, Tyler couldn't remember a damn thing, including his own name.

She licked and sucked, pulling him all the way to the back of her throat, deeper than he'd imagined she would, and he'd had plenty of fucking dreams about *this*. Then she used her hand along with her mouth, and he saw stars.

His hips jerked in time to her persistent suckling. She alternated grazing him with her teeth, slicking her tongue over his shaft, and humming around him until his body vibrated beneath her. What was supposed to be about her became about him.

She gave and gave, refusing to release him, ignoring his tap on her head, warning her to let go. He needed to be inside her with a desperation, wanting to come but not like this. But he wasn't in charge; she was.

And she was determined to control the outcome. Suck. Pump. Graze. Hum. He lost track of time and place. His balls drew up tight. He was on the verge of an explosive orgasm, and she must have known it. Felt it. Because she doubled down on her effort, and suddenly there was no stopping the surge, the volcano-like explosion that ripped through his body. He came with a shout, her name on his lips as he shuddered through the onslaught. And she stayed with him, swallowing every last drop.

His head fell against the mattress because he was so fucking spent. But he couldn't let things end here, so he forced himself to move. He flipped her off him, onto her back, and came over her. He held her down, hands on her hips, and slicked his tongue through her soaking-wet folds. Obviously taking care of him had aroused her beyond belief.

It was nearly enough to give a jolt to his well-sated cock. He dipped his head and inhaled her fragrant scent, so perfect. So Ella. And then he began to devour her, eating her up like he was a starving man at a feast. Licking and sucking her clit into his mouth until she was banging on the mattress, screaming his name.

He didn't let up, sliding his tongue over and around the sensitive nub, pausing only to insert a finger into her ready body, pumping in and out, to the jerky movements of her hips, the groans and cries coming from her lips. She'd given him the best orgasm he'd ever had short of the ones he experienced inside her body, and he intended to treat her to the same explosive completion.

He curved his finger inside her body, finding her spongy inner walls, and she shrieked, "God yes, I'm coming!" And she did, shuddering and shaking, riding out her orgasm around his hand and against his mouth. He didn't let up until he'd wrung every last contraction from her body.

Only then did he collapse to one side, wrapping himself around her, exhausted but satisfied he'd accomplished his goal. She wasn't thinking about anything except him.

Ella couldn't concentrate on work. Although she sat at her desk and attempted to make her way through her to-do list, her mind was full of everything that had gone on in the last twenty-four hours.

*I love you.* Tyler's words echoed through Ella's mind, over and over until she thought she'd go insane. It was everything she'd ever wanted to hear from him . . . and yet she couldn't respond in kind. Not until she fixed herself. And boy, did she need fixing.

Without thinking, she filled out the application, which was in her purse, stuck it in an envelope, and put it with the outgoing mail.

She picked up the phone and called information, then dialed the prison where her father was located and explained who she was, that her father was dying, and asked how she could expedite visitation. She was informed that their computer systems were down and someone would get back to her with an answer.

Her stomach hurt through the whole process of calling a state prison and being informed of the visiting rules, but she forced herself to handle it all. Because what awaited her when she came out the other side was something she'd never imagined having.

Tyler, a man who really and truly loved her. But before she could give herself to him, she needed to be whole. She needed to put the past, and the needy little girl who often crept into her adult life, behind her.

Somehow, the day crept by, and Tyler showed up as usual for the ride home. He walked in, looking sexy as always, even after a long day at work. In his charcoal slacks and white button-down shirt, he was every bit the imposing man she was falling for.

Had already fallen for, she amended, unable look away from his handsome face. And not as her best friend's older brother she had a crush on, but the caring, sensitive, often demanding adult-Tyler he'd shown her as he'd opened his heart.

On that thought, it being the first time she'd allowed herself to go there, she glanced away, not wanting him to read her emotions and feelings on her face. Instead, she organized the files and papers on her desk and rose to meet him.

"Hi there," she said, unable to stop the smile at the sight of him. Her own fears and issues be damned, this man made her feel good. So she rose to her tiptoes and brushed a kiss over his lips.

"Hi, yourself." He squeezed her waist, his eyes twinkling.

"Not that I mind you being here, and I appreciate everything you've done for me, but are we close to finding out what's going on? Who's after me?" Another thing to add to the things floating around in her head, consuming her thoughts.

His big hand on her back heated her skin. "We'll talk when we're out of here, okay?" he said, meeting her gaze.

"Okay. It's just that I hate feeling cooped up, bringing lunch, not being able to go out and get fresh air unless one of your men is following me. I want my life back," she said.

He ran his knuckles down her cheek, his warm gaze never leaving hers. "With a little luck, you'll have that soon."

"She'll have what soon?" Angie asked, striding out of her office and pausing by Ella's desk. "And who is this handsome young man?"

Ella gestured to Tyler. "Angie Crighton, this is Tyler Dare. Tyler, this is my boss."

Angie held out her manicured hand, her bangle bracelets jingling with the movement. "It's lovely to meet you, Mr. Dare."

"Likewise," he said, looking Angie over in a very orchestrated, practiced manner, and Ella couldn't help wondering what he saw beyond the cultured, refined, elegantly dressed woman.

"Are you Ella's young man?" Angie asked.

"He's—"

"I'd like to think so," Tyler said in a firm voice, cutting her off. "Ella just likes to keep her private life . . . private. So I understand your trip to St. Lucia was a success?"

Angie nodded, smoothing a hand over her platinum-colored hair, which had been pulled into a tight bun. "A very successful photo shoot."

Ella agreed. "The pictures came out fabulous."

"And we've gotten great placement in the spring maga-zines," Angie said, sounding as pleased and proud as she had when she'd congratulated Ella on her role in securing the ads.

"Did you buy any good souvenirs?" Tyler asked Angie, caus-ing Ella to narrow her gaze. "Unfortunately, whatever Ella pur-chased was stolen during the mugging, but I understand the island is known for their beads and jewelry?"

Clearly, he knew something more than Ella did, and she wondered why he was not-so-subtly questioning her boss.

"Really? I wouldn't know," Angie murmured. "We were so busy shooting the entire time, I had no time to shop."

"That's too bad." Tyler folded his arms over his chest. "I would bet an island like St. Lucia has gorgeous items. If you know where to look."

Angie's eyes narrowed to slits. She actually glared at Tyler before glancing at her watch. "It was nice meeting you, Mr. Dare, but I have a phone call I must make." She quickly turned away and rushed back into her private office, slamming the door behind her.

"Hmm," Tyler said. "It was almost as if she couldn't get away fast enough."

Ella retrieved her purse and hung the strap over her shoul-der. "Angie is eccentric," she said in a low whisper. "But you were digging. What's going on?"

He grasped her elbow and led her out of the office and onto the street. As usual, the humid air hit her as soon as she exited. "I'll tell you more when we're in the car," he said.

She waited, impatient and curious, until they were locked inside his vehicle, and she turned to face him. "Well?"

He blew out a long breath.

"What is it?" she asked, hating being in the dark.

He shrugged. "According to Luke, your boss has been involved in shady black-market deals. She's bought stolen jewelry and sold it for an obscene profit. Her name is well-known in certain circles."

"Angie?" she asked, processing the information and immediately denying it. "No." Ella dismissed the possibility with a wave of her hand. "She's impatient and, as I said, eccentric, but a thief? It's just not possible."

Tyler shot her a sympathetic look. "Luke is the best at what he does. If he says she's dealing in stolen goods, she is."

Ella glanced out the window at people walking by on the sidewalk. Ella wrinkled her nose, trying to imagine her older boss dealing with the kind of people necessary for illegal transactions. And couldn't.

"Tyler, look, I understand you need to check all angles, but Angie?" She was cut off from saying more by the ring of his cell.

He hit the answer button, allowing the call to go to speakerphone in the car. "Dare here."

"It's Luke. The cops picked up someone lurking outside Ella's apartment. They took him down to the local precinct."

Goose bumps rose on her skin, and she shivered, but not from the car's AC, which Tyler had turned on.

"Finally, a real lead," he muttered.

"You going to the police station?" Luke asked.

"Damn straight." Tyler disconnected the call and turned to Ella. "I want to head down there and see what this guy knows. Are you up to it?" he asked, squeezing her thigh.

"Damn straight," she said, meeting his gaze with a firm nod.

He grinned and pulled out of the parking spot. A little while later, Ella sat in the police station in a wooden chair, Tyler beside her, waiting for the arresting officer to arrive and speak to them.

Neither of them spoke, so she focused on the busy precinct, so many people bustling past them she lost track, and she took to studying the dingy beige walls before, finally, a young, uniformed officer walked over.

"Ms. Shaw?" he asked.

She nodded, jumping up from her seat. "I'm Ella Shaw."

"Officer DeCarlo," he said, extending his arm, and they shook hands. He glanced at Tyler, standing possessively close beside her.

Ella cleared her throat. "This is Tyler Dare. Can you tell me what happened?"

He inclined his head toward Tyler before continuing. "Let's talk over here." He gestured for them to follow, and they walked over to an empty desk, where Ella seated herself in one folding chair. Tyler leaned against the wall, arms crossed over his chest, and the officer took his seat.

Officer DeCarlo glanced at the papers on his desk, then looked up at Ella. "Someone in your building called in a suspicious guy loitering outside. We picked up a man with dark hair, a"—he glanced down as if to confirm—"Diego Santana, and took him in for questioning. I also pulled records that indicate your apartment was the subject of an attempted burglary a few weeks ago, so we were working that angle when we questioned him."

Tyler braced a hand on the back of Ella's chair and asked, "What did he have to say?"

"Considering the outstanding warrant and the fact that a search shows he'd just returned from St. Lucia, the same day you did, he was happy to talk." The officer smiled at the question, his white teeth gleaming against his tanned skin.

Ella clenched and unclenched her fists, nauseous at the reminder of her ordeal there and how it had truly followed her back here. "Is he the guy who mugged me?"

Tyler placed a hand on her shoulder, steadying her. As usual, she was grateful for his presence and support.

"Yeah." The officer scratched his head. "But we can't get him for that attack since it took place out of the country. But apparently, he was looking for a piece of hot jewelry."

"Excuse me?" Ella asked, unsure she'd heard correctly.

"Apparently he was looking for stolen jewels from a museum on the island."

Ella's stomach twisted painfully. "Stolen?" The word came out a croak, and it was no wonder. The hotel clerk had told her a story about a stolen necklace that looked very much like the one her boss had given her for safekeeping.

She didn't want to think that Angie would do something that would endanger her in any way, but it seemed like when it came to Angie, Ella's instincts were totally wrong. Tyler's and Luke's were right on target.

Officer DeCarlo met her gaze, clearly assessing her. "Yes. He claims he's working with a group who wants to return the piece to the museum and the people of St. Lucia," the dark-haired man said.

"Then why didn't he go to the police on the island? Why mug Ella?" Tyler asked.

The other man shrugged. "He says there were so many duplicate necklaces floating around, the island police would never have believed that a female tourist got her hands on the real one."

"What female tourist?" Tyler asked in a tight voice.

"He thinks you have the necklace," the officer said, pointing at Ella.

Her mouth ran dry, and she had to force the words out. "I do."

"Ella," Tyler barked, a definite warning note in his voice. He wanted her to keep quiet, but she couldn't.

"No. I have the necklace. My boss gave it to me on St. Lucia for safekeeping. When I finally returned home, I offered to return it the day I went back to work, but she said to keep it until she needed it."

With a narrowed gaze, the officer studied her. "And where is the necklace now?" he finally asked.

"In the safe in my apartment. But I didn't steal it," she rushed to add.

But clearly Angie had.

Ella had a good many emotions to sort through. She'd worked with Angie for the last two years, and the woman, though odd at times, had never been anything but supportive of Ella and her career, as well as her life. She'd traveled with Angie to many foreign places. They'd talked. Ella had learned from her. Trusted her. Looked up to her, even.

"Your boss's name?" the suspicious cop asked.

Ella hung her head and sighed. "I don't want to believe she knew about this."

"Well, then give me her name, and we'll find out."

Tyler tightened his hand on her shoulder. "Angie's being involved is the only thing that explains why someone mugged you, took your bag, and when they didn't find what they wanted, broke into your hotel room."

"I know," she said, defeated and hurt as reality set in.

Officer DeCarlo watched them with a wary expression.

"And didn't the desk clerk mention there being a necklace that looked like yours that had been stolen from a museum?" Tyler asked, repeating what she'd already thought about . . . and nailing the final head into her boss's proverbial coffin.

"She did. I just forgot all about it and never looked up the information." Ella looked up at him, Angie's betrayal sitting like lead in her stomach. "She obviously knew it was stolen when she gave it to me for safekeeping. And had me keep it so no one here would look to her for it. She was protecting *herself*."

"At your expense," Tyler muttered.

"I'm still waiting for a name," DeCarlo reminded them.

Ella sighed. "Angie Crighton."

He made a note on a piece of paper, mumbling something to himself. "That is the name our perp gave us as the original buyer of the necklace. Your boss made it clear to the people she hired to sell it she didn't intend to keep the necklace in her possession. As her assistant, you were the obvious holder of the prized piece."

"God, I'm going to be sick," Ella said, her head spinning with all she'd learned.

"Come on," Tyler said. "I'll take you home." He eyed the officer, as if daring the man to contradict him.

Ella rose on shaking legs. She thought the officer believed her, but the fact remained she was in possession of stolen property.

The uniformed cop met her gaze. "I'm going to have an officer follow you and pick up the necklace."

She nodded. "Of course."

"And we're going to check out your story more thoroughly. And we have a squad car picking up Ms. Crighton as we speak. But until we cross our *t*'s and dot our *i*'s . . . please don't leave town, and be available for questioning."

Even as Tyler pulled her close, her stomach twisted at his words, no matter how understandable.

They headed out of the police station and ran directly into Angie, being led into the station, accompanied by her own uniformed police officer.

Ella dug her heels in and stopped walking. "Angie!" Ella said, her fear and apprehension turning into anger and hurt.

The older woman spun at Ella's voice, the color draining from her face at the sight of her. The officer stood close. "This way, ma'am."

"Wait, please." Ella strode over to her boss, grateful for the chance to confront her. "Angie, how could you? You gave me a stolen necklace to transport out of the country?"

"It's not what it looks like."

"It never is," Tyler said, sarcasm lacing his tone.

Officer DeCarlo walked over, stepping up beside Ella. "I don't think this is a good idea. Frank, take her to holding A."

"Are you telling me you didn't know it was stolen?" Ella asked, ignoring the policeman beside her. "What about after I was mugged? You didn't think to tell me then? Or when my room was ransacked and I called you first chance I got? Or what about when I offered to give it back to you?" Ella asked, stepping into Angie's personal space. "How could you make me a target?" she asked, horrified when tears popped into her eyes.

For the first time since she'd known her, Angie was speechless. "Ma'am? Let's go." Her cop tugged on her arm, pulling her away from Ella.

Ella exhaled a long breath, not feeling particularly satisfied as, of course, Angie hadn't incriminated herself.

And then, just as she turned to go home, she heard a man's voice. "That's her!"

Ella pivoted. The guy with dark hair who'd been watching her when she was shopping in Miami stood, handcuffed and accompanied by an officer. But he was looking at Angie. "That's the original buyer."

And somehow, Ella had her confirmation. She'd been set up by a woman she'd trusted.

The other uniformed cop led a silent, stone-faced Angie away while the guy who'd stalked her had already been removed from the room.

"Come on, sweet girl. Let's go home." Tyler urged her toward the door with a hand around her waist.

"Wait. Officer DeCarlo?" She turned toward him.

"Yes?" he asked.

"Will she go to jail?" Ella asked.

He ran a hand through his cropped hair and shrugged. "To be frank? It's a clusterfuck. We've got the guy on attempted robbery and a few other things here, but your boss? The theft took place outside the US. We'll call in the Feds. Sorry I can't be more helpful."

Ella shook her head. "You told me what I needed to know. Thank you."

"There's an officer waiting outside to follow you home for the necklace," he said.

She nodded. "I'm ready," she said to Tyler.

As he escorted her out of the police station, she thought back to this morning, when she'd believed her life was already complicated. Now? She had all those things plus she now had no job.

# Chapter Twelve

Tyler woke up at his usual time, ready for work. He expected to find Ella fast asleep, since he usually needed to wake her up. She wasn't a morning person, and it'd taken a while, but eventually he'd discovered the best way to rouse her was with sensual, slow kisses all over her body. He looked forward to those wake-ups and was surprised, after yesterday's excitement, that she'd woken up on her own.

He rolled over, climbed out of bed, and made his way to the kitchen, hoping to find her there. He discovered her sitting at the table, drinking a cup of coffee . . . with her packed suitcase waiting against the wall.

His stomach dropped at the unexpected sight. "Going somewhere?" he asked, barely recognizing his own voice.

He understood the threat against her was over, but after all they'd been through together, he'd figured she'd at least talk to him first. Instead, she'd sucker-punched him, and he deserved better.

"I just thought, since whoever was after me has been arrested, that it was time to go home." She placed her mug on the table and rose to her feet.

With her dressed in jeans and a T-shirt and him in his boxer-briefs, he felt at a distinct disadvantage during this conversation. Or, he thought, maybe it was an advantage.

He wasn't going to let her go without a fight and met her halfway across the room. "Ella—"

Before he could gather his thoughts, she spoke. "I don't want to go, Tyler. I have to," she said, looking up at him with sad eyes.

His finger drifted down her cheek. "Explain. Because I didn't ask you to leave." He didn't want her to go.

She bit down on her trembling lower lip before she drew a deep breath and began to explain. "You said you loved me and—"

"It scared you." He cursed himself for letting that slip, jumping the gun on admitting his feelings.

"No. It was everything I ever wanted to hear, but . . ."

His heart beat faster with her initial words, then slowed to a stop with that one damned word. "But what?"

"I'm not ready." She stepped away from him, as if she needed space, and he respected her wishes, remaining in place.

Even though she was shattering his heart with every word. "What will make you ready?" he asked, grabbing on to the back of the nearest chair.

"You have your life all figured out. Your professional life as well as your personal one. You confronted your demons when you dealt with your father, and I haven't done the same thing. I don't know how to give you what you deserve when I'm distrustful of anything good and lasting in my life."

He stepped forward, breaching the distance between them, and grabbed her around the waist. If there ever was a time to use any advantage, this was it. He pulled her against him, aligning their bodies, allowing her to feel how much he desired her and always would.

"What makes you so sure seeing your father again will fix whatever you think is lacking inside you?"

She lifted her hands, let them hover in the air before finally letting them rest on his chest, her cool touch branding his skin. "I don't know that it will," she admitted, fitting herself against him, and he pulled her into a tight embrace.

His heart beat heavily against his chest, the fear of losing her winding its way through his veins until he grew cold. Panicked.

But if there was one thing he knew, he couldn't force her to stay. He had to hope she would come to terms with her demons and return to him on her own.

He kissed the top of her head and released her.

She stumbled back, surprised. "What's wrong?"

"I'm doing what you asked," he said, forcing the words out from the darkest part of his soul. "I'm letting you go."

He prayed he wasn't making the biggest mistake of his life. But he wanted all of Ella, unconditionally, and the only way she could give him that was to make peace with her own past—even though it killed him to let her walk out his door.

Word spread among the Dare siblings that Tyler needed a guys' night out. He had no doubt Avery was the source of the rumor. Who else would know that Ella had returned home and informed the rest of the clan?

So despite his mood, he found himself with his brothers, staring at delicious-smelling Italian food at Ian's favorite restaurant, Emilio's. His brothers ate like they hadn't been fed in a year, inhaling pasta and chicken parmigiana, while Tyler focused on his third scotch of the evening. Tyler merely watched the two of them with some level of amusement. Not much considering his mood.

"I can't believe you finished the chicken," Ian said to Scott, who was reaching for the utensils to give himself more pasta. "Touch that ziti and I'll stab you with my fork," he said. "Leave some for me."

Scott scowled at him, not moving his hand. "You already ate double what I ate."

"How do your wives put up with you?" Tyler asked.

At that, Ian focused on Tyler and pinned him with a glare. "Riley loves me."

And while Ian was looking at Tyler, Scott stole what was left of the dish, stabbing the pasta with his fork and landing it on his plate.

"Fuck," Ian muttered and gestured for the waiter, ordering another main course of chicken parm. "That's for you," he said, pointing to Tyler. "You need to eat," he said, acting like the head of the family he was and had been for years.

"He's right," Scott said. "Starving won't bring Ella back."

It was Tyler's turn to scowl. "We're not discussing her."

Ian cocked his head to one side. "We wouldn't have to if you'd done what I told Alex once."

"What would that be?" Tyler was sorry he asked before he even finished the sentence.

With a shrug, Ian said, "A little bondage wouldn't hurt. Tie her to the bed until she accepts who's boss." A smirk lifted the corners of his brother's mouth just as Tyler and Scott both let out a loud chuckle.

"What's so funny?"

"You might have been in charge once upon a time, but we all know Riley wears the pants in the family," Tyler said through laughter he hadn't thought he was capable of min- utes earlier.

Damn, but he loved his family. They'd left their spouses to make sure he was okay and take his mind off his problems.

"The day you tie Riley up and tell her what to do, I'll—"

"I'd cool it if I were you. You do not want to discuss my sex life," Ian said.

Tyler rolled his eyes. "I sure as hell don't." Not when he wasn't getting any and wouldn't for who knew how long.

"Me neither."

"Well, then. That's settled." Ian placed his fork onto the table and took a long sip of his own drink, which matched Tyler's. "How about we discuss the fact that you let your woman walk out the door?"

A slow-building throb began in Tyler's temple. "Really? We're going there?"

"Well, she went to visit her father in prison, so would you like to begin there instead?" Scott asked.

The pounding in Tyler's head turned into a full-fledged stabbing pain. Somehow, between her shocking him with the announcement that she was leaving and dealing with letting her go, he'd forgotten she'd had that letter to deal with.

"When? And how the fuck do you know?" he asked, glaring at Scott. Even if he was grateful, no need to let the smug bastard know it.

He shrugged. "Avery called Meg to ask how her nephew is doing, and she mentioned it. She left tonight so she could stay over at a motel and be there first thing in the morning."

"Where?" Tyler barked out.

"Sorry, man. I don't know and neither does Meg." Scott gave him a sympathetic look as he answered. "And before you kill me, I found out on the way over here when she called me and told me. It's a done deal. You'll have to wait until she gets back to talk to her."

Tyler rubbed at his temples, his emotions close to bubbling over.

"How is Cole?" Ian asked Scott, correctly guessing Tyler did not want to continue the conversation about Ella in any way.

He had too much to think about on his own. And as his brothers discussed Meg's breastfeeding, baby Cole's diapers, and Ian's daughter's tantrums, somehow, Tyler formulated a plan.

He wasn't sure if Ella would appreciate it, but he couldn't live with himself if he didn't execute it with the precision of a well-run operation worthy of his days in the army.

Ella thought back on how things with Tyler had ended. He'd let her go much more easily than she'd thought he would . . . and Ella wasn't sure how she felt about that. Grateful that he'd respected her wishes? Hurt that he hadn't argued? Surprised? All of the above, she thought, but she was unable to deny he'd given her what she'd said she needed. And something told her he always would.

Which didn't change the fact that she was alone in her apartment just as she'd wanted—and miserable without Tyler. It had hurt to leave him, but if they were going to make it as a couple over the long term, she had to take the necessary steps to get her life together and put her past behind her.

She slept alone in her double bed, rolling over, reaching for Tyler in the middle of the night, only to wake up in a dark room on the wrong side of her small mattress. His bedroom had a roomy king, not that they'd used the extra space. They'd usually slept wrapped around one another in the middle of his bed. She didn't even mind the body heat he'd generated because he'd been there, by her side.

He'd taken care of her, looked out for her, and she liked to think she'd done the same for him. Or at least she'd tried to be there when he'd needed her, when Olivia was in distress and when he'd had to deal with his father's unexpected appearance. She hoped it was enough for him to know how much she cared, even if she couldn't be with him now.

The following morning arrived, leaving her exhausted from very little sleep. And when she attempted to eat breakfast, she remembered her refrigerator was empty, which meant she had to visit the supermarket, a chore she hated, but which hadn't been so awful when she'd gone with Tyler. She had plenty of time to browse the aisles . . . seeing as how she was unemployed.

Another thing she did over the next few days was call around to contacts in the business and put out feelers indicating she was looking for employment. She didn't have any immediate luck in the job search, but the Miami fashion industry was small, and she let the right people know she was interested. She just didn't know how long it would take to find a new job.

Good thing she had a nest egg in her savings account, she thought. She wasn't a big spender, her childhood having taught her the value of being careful with her money.

She also counted her blessings that the police had merely confiscated the necklace Angie had given her to hold instead of arresting her for possession of stolen property. Thanks to the man they'd arrested recognizing Angie and the resulting confession when her boss had broken down in custody, the cops had all the evidence they needed. Officer DeCarlo had called her early that morning to fill her in and thank her for her willingness to cooperate.

To her surprise, he'd asked her out. She couldn't believe it. One minute he was telling her not to leave town, and the next, he was asking her on a date. But she wasn't a free agent, no matter that she'd left Tyler behind. She was a woman in need of freeing herself.

Her cell phone rang, and the name of the prison showed on the screen. She answered and was informed she was approved for expedited visitation, and the person told her she should come soon, indicating, without saying as much, her father didn't have much time left.

Her throat filled, and her eyes watered at the finality of it all. She grabbed a piece of paper and wrote down the hours again, just to be sure she didn't forget.

The trip would take her five hours there and five back, so she'd have to stay overnight. On her laptop, she then looked into motels in the area and made a reservation, deciding to leave by three p.m. that day.

The drive was long and boring, with too much time to think, but the motel wasn't bad as motels went. And she managed to sleep a few fitful hours.

Come morning, she dressed in a subdued outfit to match her mood. Tan pants and a white collared shirt, buttoned up, little makeup, no jewelry, so she felt comfortable no matter who she ran into at the prison. She pulled her hair into a low ponytail and secured it with a hair tie.

She hadn't seen her father since she was a teenager, and she wasn't sure what to expect today, especially since he'd said he had cancer and she'd been encouraged to rush her visit.

How progressed was his illness? How frail and sick did he look? Her stomach flipped with nerves, and she couldn't manage to eat breakfast. Not even a cup of coffee for courage. Instead, she tossed a protein bar in her purse for later, grabbed her keys, and headed out.

She approached the prison. The barbed wire made her stomach cramp, and she gripped the steering wheel harder. A guard verified her at the gate, and she went through the process, numb as she was scanned and patted down, her small purse emptied out and thoroughly checked.

A little while later, she was escorted down bare, gray cinderblock halls, toward what she was told was an infirmary.

The guard paused outside a locked door with a small window. She glanced inside, catching sight of an inmate lying in a hospital bed. He was bald, his coloring gray, and he was so frail. He turned his head. She knew he couldn't see her—yet—but she was taken aback. Because although she recognized the man in the bed as her father, after the split second of identification, she realized she didn't *know* him at all.

"Ready?" the guard asked.

As she'd ever be, she thought and nodded. He unlocked the door, the sound of the dead bolt reverberating around and inside her. He opened the door and gestured for her to walk inside.

He accompanied her, standing by the wall, his gaze never wavering.

Her father's gaze, watery and sad, locked with hers, and she walked slowly over to the bed. "Hi," she said, having a hard time finding her voice. A harder time calling him *Dad*.

"Hi, princess."

She flinched at the childhood name she hadn't heard in . . . what felt like forever. Not since before he'd remarried.

"Thank you for coming."

She managed a nod. "I'm sorry you're sick."

His lips thinned into a line. "It's nothing more or less than what I deserve. For what I did, not just for driving drunk and killing that poor man, but for what I did to you."

Her throat was too full to speak, so she merely shook her head, gathering her composure and ability to talk. She cleared her throat. "You don't . . ." She swallowed hard. "I forgive you," she said, knowing it was true.

And the reason was that this man wasn't her father. The man who'd married a cold, unlovable woman wasn't her daddy. Nor was the man who'd begged his ten-year-old to give bone marrow to his wife. And what had come after? That broken shell of a man wasn't the man who'd loved her so hard or so well.

He'd died the day he'd married Janice in order to forget the pain of losing his wife.

"Ella, I—"

"No. Don't say anything. Please." She didn't want to hear it. Didn't want to relive anything or remember the past. "Let forgiveness be enough."

She reached out for his worn, leathery hand. Sadness filled her, but oddly, she didn't feel the loss the way she'd thought she would. She'd already grieved, mourned, lived with the emptiness her entire life.

"Thank you," he said.

She nodded, not letting go. She sat with him until he fell asleep, then watched him for a while more.

Finally she rose to her feet. And with one last glance, she nodded to the guard and headed *home*.

It wasn't easy for Tyler to sit back and wait for Ella to return from her visit to her father. Everything in him wanted to head to the prison and be there when she faced him in person. Unfortunately, he knew better than to make the trip.

He didn't know where she was staying, and he couldn't get into the penitentiary, but he had the resources to take care of those things. But the more rational side of his brain prevailed, reminding him that Ella wouldn't appreciate his interference.

From the minute he'd stormed back into her life, the one thing she'd made clear was that she was used to handling things on her own. If he wanted a future with her—and he damned well did—then he had to prove he respected her independence. Once he managed that, he had plans to teach her a lesson for shutting him out. From then on, they'd be a team, and he knew just how to make that point.

But first, he needed her to return from her trip.

After the arrest outside her apartment building, he figured her neighbors would freak if they saw a strange guy sleeping in his SUV, waiting for her to show up. Instead, he planned. He checked prison visiting hours and assumed she'd be there for a nine a.m. visit. An hour inside, a five-hour drive home, give or take. So he planted himself in a visitor's spot at two thirty p.m. to be safe. He didn't want to miss her and delay what he planned on being a reunion.

These couple of days without her had been long enough.

He wasn't sure how long he sat in the truck, window open, humidity slamming him in the face, trying not to doze off. He'd had little sleep the night before, worrying about how Ella would handle the visit, from the prison frisking to facing her dad. He reminded himself that she was stronger than she looked and had proven that to herself and to him over and over again.

Finally, her white car pulled into the lot and turned into her spot, across from where he'd parked. He exited his SUV and leaned against the truck's back end, arms folded across his chest while he waited for her to notice him.

He heard her car door slam, and she headed toward the building. She looked tired, dark circles under her eyes and tear stains on her cheeks, but still beautiful in his eyes. She appeared fragile—she wasn't—but he still wanted to pull her into his arms, protect her, and never let her go.

First he had to convince her they were stronger together than apart.

She fumbled through her purse as she walked, not noticing him until she'd almost reached the front door of the apartment building.

"Hey," he said.

"Tyler!" She stopped short and met his gaze, surprise in her exhausted expression, followed quickly by a pleased smile.

Not a bad start, he thought, considering she'd been the one to walk away from him.

"What are you doing here?" she asked.

"I've been waiting for you to get home."

"Oh. I was—" She cut herself off, and he'd bet she didn't want to tell him where she'd gone. Alone. "Were you here long?" she asked him instead.

"I know where you were," he said, unable to keep the concern from his voice. "Word travels fast in my family."

She sighed. "Avery told you."

"Indirectly, yes."

She shook her head, clearly not surprised. "Well, if you're going to yell at me for visiting the prison alone, let's get out of this ridiculous humidity first."

Clearly she knew him well. But he didn't plan on yelling. Much. He inclined his head, and they stepped toward the door. He opened it for her and followed her up to her apartment, then inside. She placed her purse on the counter and flopped onto the sofa, completely wiped out.

He settled in by her side. "So how'd it go?" he asked.

She turned her head toward him, still resting against the back of the sofa, meeting his gaze. "It was sad. He's obviously dying, and that hurts to see, but . . ." She trailed off, biting down on her lower lip.

He gave her some time, and when she didn't continue, he nudged her with his knee. "But what?"

She lifted her head and curled her legs beneath her, facing him directly. "I don't want you to think I'm cold or unfeeling but . . . I didn't know the man I went to see. He wasn't my dad. Not the man who loved me when I was younger."

She rubbed her hands along her arms, and he ached to pull her into his. But she needed to tell him her story, and he had to give her the time to do it.

"I think . . . no, I know that I mourned him already." Her eyes filled as she spoke, and Tyler waited patiently, here for her if she needed him. "I lost my father when he remarried, and every time he did something to hurt me, I grieved again. Over and over until I shut off my feelings and learned to cope on my own."

Unable to keep from touching her, he grasped her hand and ran his thumb over her wrist, extending his support the only way he could.

"I can understand that," he said, thinking about his own life. "That's how I feel about my father," he admitted. "I don't know him anymore and haven't since that day I walked in on him with Savannah when I was fourteen years old."

She smiled at him. "I figured you'd get it. The thing is, I spent all these years feeling angry at him and hurt. And all that did was impact my own life. I resented him, and I didn't like myself much." She shook her head, her sadness palpable. "While driving home, I thought back over my life, and I realized I cut myself off from people. From joy and happiness, afraid everyone would hurt me the way he did."

"Except Avery," Tyler said.

She nodded. "Except Avery . . . and until you."

His breath hitched. Stopped. Then started again, along with the rapid beating of his heart. He didn't want to read too much into those three words, but the organ inside his chest, the one she already owned, wasn't listening.

"Avery came into my life when I was the loneliest. She's a part of me. But you . . ." She scooted closer to him, bracing her hands on either side of his face, and met his gaze. "You're the other half of my heart. You always have been."

"Ella," he said on a groan, raising his hand, cupping the back of her neck tighter, their lips inches apart.

"I just needed to grow up and put the past behind me," she whispered.

"We both needed to do that."

"I'm sorry I left you," she said, wrapping her arms around his neck and kissing him on the lips, too briefly because they weren't finished talking.

"I'm not. You did what you needed to in order to come back to me whole. But you went to the prison by yourself." He disentangled her arms, holding on to her wrists in front of her as he spoke. "You visited your father by yourself." He shook his head. "What did I tell you when we returned from St. Lucia?"

She slicked her tongue over her lips, letting him know she'd caught his deliberate stony tone of voice and was nervous.

"Well?" he asked.

"You told me that I don't have to be alone anymore."

"Right. I said you don't have to be alone anymore," he repeated, and they each grinned.

But he sobered faster. "You had to know that no matter what happened between us, I'd have gone with you." He'd do anything for her, and he needed her not just to know that but to believe it.

She blinked rapidly. "But I needed—"

"To do it alone," he said, his jaw tight at those damned words. "Now let's get something straight. That is the last time I want to hear you say that. Do you love me?"

The question shocked him when it came out of his mouth. But hell, she'd said he was the other half of her heart. What else could she have meant? Still, he needed to hear those words in order to make his point.

She stared at him through widened hazel eyes, drew a deep breath, and nodded. "I do. I love you."

"And you know I love you. Now we go forward together. Agreed?" he asked.

She smiled, for the first time since her return, the happy emotion reaching her eyes. "Agreed."

"Good." He rose and pulled her to her feet.

"Where are we going?" she asked.

Without answering, he lifted her up and into his arms, and she squealed, a move and a sound that were coming to be among his favorites.

She slid her arms around his neck, her fingers gliding into his hair. The simple touch sent his senses reeling, his cock hardening, his arousal intense. And probably permanent whenever she was around.

"From now on, you're going to let me take care of you the way I want to."

"We'll see," she taunted him, treating him to a teasing grin.

He laughed. "You're bad," he said as he deposited her onto the bed.

"No." She became much more serious. "I'm *yours.*"

He came down over her, sealing his mouth over hers and sliding his tongue along the seam of her lips. She moaned and opened for him, tangling her tongue with his. The kiss went on and on. And knowing he had her not just in his arms but in his life forever, Tyler was content to kiss her forever.

# Epilogue

To celebrate the marriage of Emma St. Claire and Michael Brooks, the Dare siblings gathered at a ballroom far from Robert Dare's hotels, a beautiful room decorated in white and gold and an outdoor terrace large enough to hold the entire extended family and friends.

Ian Dare stood alone by the table set aside for immediate family, looking over his siblings and his mother with pride.

Riley, the love of Ian's life, had held his three-year-old daughter's hand as she'd walked down the aisle. His wife was a vision in a gold gown, his adorable little girl a pouf of white dress as she'd giggled her way to dropping flower petals down the aisle. He'd watched, his heart full to bursting, the same way it was now as his entire family laughed and smiled.

All settled. All happy. All having overcome the main obstacle thrown in their path, Robert Dare's betrayal. Watching his family now, Ian thought, his role in their lives was complete. He'd stepped up, taken over, and made certain each one of them had everything they needed. He'd never considered it at his own expense, but once Riley had burst past his well-built defenses, he'd realized how precarious life was. How easily he might have pushed her away instead of pursuing her, and missed out on the family he now had.

Nobody knew, but Riley was pregnant again. They didn't want to reveal the news and spoil his mother's special day.

Of course, Emma would think another grandbaby was her wedding present, but he and Riley wanted to keep the news to themselves awhile longer.

He whispered a prayer of thanks that his brothers had found what Ian had. A woman who could share life's burdens and joys. He'd never considered himself sentimental, but after watching Scott and Tyler fall over themselves not to let their women get away, Ian patted himself on the back for the example he'd set going after Riley.

And then there were his sisters. His pride and joy. Olivia and Avery, for whom Ian would kill to protect, had also finally put their father's betrayal behind them enough to open their hearts to good men.

Ian shrugged, and while he was at it, he patted himself on the back for that too. He grinned and looked over as his mother and Michael danced in the corner, lost in their own world. He couldn't take credit for their happiness, but he was damned glad his mother could have a second chance after raising her kids. Because no doubt about it, she was the driving force behind the people they'd all become.

"What are you grinning at?" Ian turned toward a man he hadn't seen in years, Kaden Barnes, software billionaire and one of his college friends. Kade was in town for a business meeting with Ian, and true to her giving nature, Emma was all too happy to invite his old friend to her wedding.

"I'm just taking in the changes in my family," Ian said.

Kade's gaze swept the room. "They're all paired off. Have you all lost your minds?" Kade's icy-blue eyes flashed with more seriousness than humor.

"You still haven't met the one, or you wouldn't be so quick to dismiss settling down," Ian replied.

The other man raised one dark eyebrow. "I'll take your word for it, thanks."

Ian shook his head. "Can't be because you don't have your choice of willing women. I'd bet they're all over you in the city. Hell, they were back when we were in school, and you weren't half as bulked up as you are now."

"I work out." Kade grinned, flexing his arm with an arrogant grin. "And can I help it if I've got good genes? Now I've got the personal bank account to match."

Ian knew Kade was touchy about his father's wealth and riding his daddy's coattails. He'd been determined to make it on his own and he had. He and his partners had developed a revolutionary cell phone app that'd made him wealthy beyond imagination.

Unfortunately he was involved in an ugly dispute with a fourth man that threatened everything they were building. Kaden Barnes had a lot on his plate. Maybe he really had no time for a relationship. Or maybe he was jaded.

"Wealth like yours makes it hard to tell what's real," Ian said, because he knew how that felt. Until he'd met Riley, that was.

He glanced over at his wife. Was it his imagination or did her breasts look bigger already? When she was pregnant with Rainey, they'd been large, luscious, and tasted fucking delicious. He mulled over the notion of pulling her into a private room before thinking better of it. Later tonight, he'd have her all to himself.

"Are we still on for our meeting Monday?" Kade asked, breaking into his thoughts.

Kade, along with his business partners, Derek West and Lucas Monroe, lived in New York, eschewing Silicon Valley for the Big Apple. They were all in town to recruit potential investors for when they took their company public.

Ian nodded. "Gabe's in town for the wedding, so he'll join us instead of having a separate sit-down with you in Manhattan."

Kade picked up a whiskey he'd left on a nearby table and took a long drink. "I like your cousin. We hung out often. Or at least we did until . . ."

"I got my chance with Isabelle?" Gabe asked, joining them with his beautiful wife on his arm.

"Yes, that," Kade said with an eye roll. "However, you are stunning, Mrs. Dare," he said, taking Isabelle's hand and kissing the top. "It's good to see you again."

"Oh, he's still a charmer," Isabelle mused, her brown eyes dancing with amusement.

Gabe stiffened and pulled her closer. "Hands off my wife, Barnes."

Kade laughed and raised his hands in the air. "No harm meant. I want your money more than anything else you might . . . *possess.*"

Ian grinned. Apparently Kade knew of Gabe's dominant proclivities. It ran in the Dare men's genes. Ian figured Kade, with his self-assured, cool personality, would be equally controlling with whatever woman finally tamed the bad boy he liked to claim he was.

"Kade, one of Olivia's friends would like an introduction," Ian's sister Avery said, passing by as she headed for the dance floor with Grey.

"Only if she's into one-night stands," Kade muttered under his breath, but Ian caught the low words.

"How's keeping your women at arm's length working out for you?" Isabelle asked. Obviously she'd heard him too.

Kade rolled his shoulders. "I can barely keep a secretary. I don't have the time or the inclination to try and keep a woman happy."

Isabelle shook her head and patted his arm as if he were a sad puppy.

"He'll learn," Gabe said, echoing Ian's words and thoughts.

Gabe merely smiled. "Care to dance?" he asked his wife.

She nodded and they started to walk off, arm in arm.

Kade finished off the last of his whiskey. "Something tells me I'd better have this business meeting and get the hell out of here. There's something in the water I don't want to touch," he said on a brittle laugh. "I'll catch you later," he said and strode off.

Ian met Gabe's knowing grin. Men who were in as deep denial about relationships as Kade usually fell the hardest. Ian ought to know. Same with all of his siblings.

He glanced around one last time, still pleased with how his family had settled down. Despite Robert Dare, or maybe because of the hell he'd put them all through, the Dares had grown stronger. And Ian couldn't be prouder, he thought as he finally went to join everyone to celebrate the things that truly mattered in their lives: love, family, and the future.

*The Dare Series continues with the NY Dares Series, Dare to Surrender, Book #1*

### Dare to Love Series
Book 1: *Dare to Love* (Ian & Riley)
Book 2: *Dare to Desire* (Alex & Madison)
Book 3: *Dare to Touch* (Olivia & Dylan)
Book 4: *Dare to Hold* (Scott & Meg)
Book 5: *Dare to Rock* (Avery & Grey)
Book 6: *Dare to Take* (Tyler & Ella)

### NY Dares Series
Book 1: *Dare to Surrender* (Gabe & Isabelle)
Book 2: *Dare to Submit* (Decklan & Amanda)
Book 3: *Dare to Seduce* (Max & Lucy)

The NY Dares books are more erotic/hotter books
Turn the page to start reading the *Dare to Surrender* excerpt!

# Prologue

### Gabe

Gabriel Dare eyed the beautiful woman with the bright smile that didn't reach her eyes, hoping his bland expression concealed the intense emotions she roused inside him. Protective instincts the likes of which he'd never experienced before. The desire to sweep her into his arms, breathe in her unique scent no designer could have created, and steal her away from this god-awful staid country club was strong.

He had an endless supply of beautiful women all eager to share his bed—including Naomi, his latest affair—and yet they did nothing for him except accompany him on endless nights like this one. And take the edge off his need. True satisfaction hadn't existed for him in far too long.

He was bored. Unless he was watching *her*. Then the perfection and elegance of the Hamptons club vanished, and *she* was all he saw.

Blonde hair fell down her back in less-than-perfect waves, defying the stick-straight look most women preferred. Her lush, sexy body, so unlike the females he normally bedded, had his hands itching to learn those curves and show her what true pleasure really was. She was unattainable, living with one of Wall Street's stars, but she could do so much better.

Oddly, it wasn't her lack of availability that appealed. She was bright and witty, and she could hold her own with just about anyone, making whoever she spoke to feel important. He admired that trait. They hadn't spent more than a few minutes here and there in each other's company, but she'd taken his breath away from the first look.

Gabe would do just about anything to attain something he wanted, but he drew the line at poaching on another man's territory. Still, he had to admit she tested even his willpower, and he'd had practice at being alone. He'd married young and miscalculated badly. Afterward, he'd been certain that after Krissie's death, for which he felt responsible, the smart thing would be to keep a safe emotional distance from women.

One look at Isabelle Masters and he'd changed his mind. There was something about her that filled the emptiness inside him. To the point where just watching her was enough to calm his usually restless soul. Unfortunately, they didn't run into each other nearly often enough.

Gabe ran a hand through his hair, groaning as he caught sight of Naomi making her way toward him, a cocktail plate with one celery stick and a carrot in her hand. His gaze darted to Isabelle as she crossed the room in the opposite direction, careful to avoid him as long as the man she lived with was around.

She was taken, and all he could do was admire. Look and not touch. But if she ever became available, all bets were off.

# Chapter One

## *Isabelle*

He begged me not to walk out the door. I did it anyway. The scariest part? How much I wanted to go. I'd spent years of my life fully invested in a relationship I'd thought meant everything to me. How could all the emotion disappear?

The answer came to me as I stood in the dark driveway by my car, the only light coming from the headlights of the vehicle I'd turned on with the push of a remote. The feelings had drained away, diminishing slowly from something I'd hoped would be full and wonderful at the age of twenty-two to something painfully empty by the time I'd reached twenty-five. I wasn't old, but at this moment, I felt ancient and weary down to my bones.

I glanced up just as the first drop of rain touched my face. Normally I'd pull up a hood and protect my out-of-control curly hair from frizz, worried about how I'd look to Lance and the carefully chosen people with whom he surrounded himself. He called them friends, but none knew the meaning of the word. Instead, I embraced the wildness of the storm that suddenly threatened to release from the heavens. Each warm droplet hit and spread across my cheeks, cleansing my skin and my soul. The wind took flight, lifting my hair, blowing strands onto my face, and setting the rest of me free.

"Isabelle!" Lance yelled down from the window he'd opened on the second floor of his Hamptons summer home. It had been too long since I'd considered any part of it mine. If I ever had.

I unwillingly looked up.

"You've had your tantrum. Now come back inside, and we'll talk like civilized people. You don't want to cause a scene in front of the neighbors."

*Heaven forbid*, I thought, sparing a last glance at the place I'd lived for too long. The house was Lance Daltry's show-place, just as I had been nothing more than an accessory. I may have organized his personal life and thrown obligatory dinner parties, but I'd contributed nothing of substance. He'd never allowed me to spend any of the money I'd earned before I'd quit my interior design job. Unnecessary, he'd said. If I loved him, I'd stay home and take care of the house. More like he'd wanted control, and I'd given it to him.

Luckily for me, I'd saved a good amount from those early days. Not so luckily, I'd let Lance invest my money and maintain control of those accounts. And what were the chances that money would be available for my withdrawal on Monday morning? I closed my eyes at the thought.

Although I'd been in Manhattan for a couple of years by the time I'd met Lance, I was still the naïve girl who'd taken a bus from a small town near Niagara Falls and traveled to the big city alone. Too bad I hadn't had the street smarts to peg Lance for the phony he'd turned out to be.

"Isabelle!" He yelled down to me again, not bothering to come out in the rain to talk to me, let alone apologize like a man. Not when the rain would ruin his thousand-dollar suit and hundred-dollar haircut.

*Not talking*, I thought silently and merely shook my head.

Talk was what had gotten me to remain in a relationship I knew I didn't want with a man I couldn't trust; it was what had convinced me that Lance, a Wall Street trader, was my soul mate when, in the deepest part of my heart, I knew there was no such thing. And most humiliating, talk was what had led me to believe his lies, despite knowing I wasn't truly satisfied with him or in his gilded cage.

I didn't need therapy to tell me why I'd been so susceptible to Lance's charm and desire to own me. The childhood I didn't like to think about held the answers. But having escaped him now, one thing was certain: I wasn't going back.

"Would you quit being a child and get back here?" Lance tried once more, patronizing me even though he was the one in the wrong. Another favorite ploy of his.

Shaking, I climbed into my beloved car, slamming the door and escaping Lance's tirade. I started the engine and paused, breathing in deep, the events of the last few minutes rushing through my brain like a bad film.

I'd been on our shared laptop, searching for recipes I'd stored there. Seeing a file I didn't recognize, I'd clicked. And the graphic, sexual images of a naked and sweaty Lance along with my beautiful neighbor, who'd dared to call herself my friend, had flashed on the screen. Nausea had risen at the visual proof of what I'd only suspected before.

I shivered at the memory of those images, proud of how I'd walked out without a word—or a suitcase. My body was frozen, my heart encased in ice. Although I could turn on the heated seats, the reminder of what it felt like to be numb with betrayal would keep me safe in the future.

I turned on the ignition, but surprisingly, no waterworks mixed with the dampness from the rain. Instead, adrenaline raced through my veins faster than even my beloved car could take a highway. I ought to be afraid. Panicked. Yearning to turn around and go back to the security I'd known.

My foot pressed the accelerator, and I backed out of the driveway without looking back. I might not know where I'd go or what I'd do, but I was moving forward. At last.

On the satellite radio, the 1979 Buggles song proclaimed that video killed the radio star. *Untrue*, I thought as I drove into the dark night. Radio had thrived anyway. And tonight,

though video killed my dream of living happily ever after in
a life I thought I'd carefully crafted to prevent loneliness,
those graphic sexual images of betrayal wouldn't destroy me.
Instead, they'd set me free.

### *Isabelle: Out of the Frying Pan*

I was arrested a mile outside of Manhattan. Grand theft auto,
the cop said. Bullshit, I replied. The baby Benz belonged
to me.

Still, he cuffed me and hauled me to the nearest police
station. He said his name was Officer Dare, and he was a dark-
haired man, tall, taller than Lance—who prided himself on
his height—and broader beneath his uniform, from what I
could tell. His intense expression never wavered. All seriousness, all the time, but I sensed he'd be handsome if he smiled.
So far, he hadn't.

Once inside the typical-looking police station—not that I'd
seen the inside of one before, but what I'd thought one would
look like from watching *Law & Order*—he sat me beside his
wooden desk and *cuffed* me to the desk.

I ought to be scared, but some stupid part of me had already
decided this new part of my life was some grand adventure. At
least it was until Officer Dare asked me to empty my pockets
and divested me of my last five hundred dollars, cash I'd taken
from the *extra* stash I kept in my nightstand.

He thumbed through the bulging stack of twenties in
never-ending silence.

The money represented my lifeline. "I'll need to eat when
I get out of here," I told my jailer.

He didn't look up. "You'll get it back."

"All of it?" I asked as if I seriously believed a member of
the police force would take a *down-on-her-luck* woman's chance
at food.

He set his jaw in annoyance. "We log it and count it. In
front of you. I was just about to do that . . . ma'am."

For some inane reason, I burst out laughing. I'd gone from living in denial to homeless and arrested in a ridiculously short time. This whole turn in my life really was absurd.

I rubbed my free hand up and down over one arm. "Don't I get one phone call?"

He nodded and reached for the telephone on the desk.

I frowned, suddenly realizing I had no one to call. Lance was out of the question, and *our* friends were really *his* friends. As for my parents, they didn't remember my birthday, so something told me a late-night call to pick up their daughter from jail would not be their number-one priority.

"Never mind," I said softly.

The officer stared at me, confused. "Now you don't want to use the phone?"

"No, thank you." Because I was totally, utterly alone.

Nausea rose like bile in my throat, and I dug my nails into my palms. When I forced myself to breathe deeply, the familiar burning in my chest returned, and I realized I'd walked away without the one thing I never left home without, and it wasn't my license.

"Any chance you've got some Tums?" I asked.

He ground his teeth together, and I swear I heard his molars scraping. "Okay, yeah. I'll get right on that," he muttered and strode off.

"I'll just wait here," I called back. I lifted my arm the short distance the cuffs would allow and groaned.

What felt like an endless stretch of time passed, during which I reviewed my options, of which, once again, I had none.

*Now what*, I wondered, utter and complete despair threatening for the first time. Eventually I forced back the lump in my throat and forced myself to make the best of the situation.

I kicked my feet against the linoleum floor. Leaned back in the chair and studied the cracked ceiling. Hummed along to the tune crackling on the radio in the background. And yeah, I tried not to cry.

"You know, I thought it would take me longer to get you in cuffs." A familiar masculine voice that oozed pure sin sounded beside me.

*It couldn't be*, I thought, but from the tingling in my body, I already knew it was. "Gabriel Dare, what brings you into this part of Mayberry?"

He chuckled, a deeply erotic sound that matched his mention of the handcuffs, but he didn't answer my question.

Left with no choice, I tipped my head and looked into his self-possessed, dark-blue eyes. Eyes too similar to my cop, and suddenly the last name registered. In an unfamiliar place and time, my mind on my arrest and nothing more, I hadn't made the connection before.

I knew Gabriel Dare from the country club Lance belonged to, but despite the upper-crust connection, there was nothing similar about the two men. Where Lance was sandy-haired and a touch Waspish in looks, Gabe, as his friends called him, possessed thick, dark-sable hair and roguish good looks.

Gabe's very posture and demeanor set him apart from any other man I'd met. His white teeth, tanned skin, and chiseled features were put together in a way that made him extraordinarily handsome. That he owned the space and air around him merely added to his appeal. An appeal that had never been lost on me, not even now, shackled as I was to a desk in a police station.

His stare never wavered, those navy eyes locked on me, and if I hadn't been sitting, I'd be in a puddle at his feet.

"You look good cuffed," he said in a deliciously low voice.

Immediate thoughts of me bound and at his mercy assaulted me. My body, which hadn't been worshiped well in far too long, if ever, had been taken over by the notion of Gabe, his strong touch playing me with an expert hand.

I squeezed my thighs together, but instead of easing, the ache only grew. Heat rushed through me at a rapid pace, my breasts heavy, my sex pulsing in a dull throbbing that begged to be filled. I blinked hard in an impossible attempt to center myself.

He grinned, as if he'd heard every naughty thought in my head.

It had always been this way between us. Any time I ran into him at the club, the attraction had been electric, and when we found ourselves alone, the flirting outrageous.

One night, Gabe had caught me exiting the ladies' room. Lance had come upon us then, and once home, he'd accused me of desiring Gabe. I'd denied it, of course.

I'd lied.

Lance knew it, and after catching us talking privately at more than one event, he'd kept a firm lock on my arm. And because I desperately wanted the life I'd chosen to make sense, I'd allowed the possession.

Besides, Gabe always had an elegant woman on his arm, a different one each time. He could have any beautiful female he desired. Why would he choose me? Even Lance, who I'd been with for what felt like a lifetime, liked ownership, not *me*. And let's face it, my parents hadn't wanted me either. So believing in myself wasn't my strong suit.

"So. What are you in for?" Gabe settled in his brother's chair, propping an elbow on the cluttered desk so he could lean closer. "Prostitution?"

"Excuse me?" I choked out. "You know I'm not a hooker!" I said, offended, the whispers I'd heard when Lance and I had first gotten together rushing back.

*Gold digger* and *mistress* were among the chosen words, never mind that Lance's single-minded pursuit had broken down every one of my defenses.

Gabe chuckled, assuring me he'd been joking. "Seriously, you dress down as well as you dress up." His gaze raked over me, hot approval in the inky depths, appreciating me in a way Lance never had.

My insides trembled at the overwhelming effect this man had on me. "Where's the cop with my money?" I asked, glancing around.

"Worried about your stash?" Gabe drummed his fingers on the desk. "Are you sure you're not a hooker?" he mused.

I didn't want to grin, but I did. "Why are you so desperate to think I am? Are you a pimp or something?"

He burst out laughing, the sound echoing through the walls of the quiet station. "Not quite," he said, obviously amused.

The tread of his brother's heavy footsteps announced his return.

Gabe looked at the other man with a disappointed expression. "Bro, didn't anyone tell you you're supposed to handcuff a lady to the headboard, not a desk?" He folded his arms across his broad chest. "It's no wonder you can't get any action."

I ducked my head, trying not to laugh.

A flush highlighted the other man's cheeks. "What are you doing here, and why are you bothering my suspect?"

Gabe tapped on his wristwatch. Gold. White face. Rolex. All my jewelry was in Lance's safe, I realized, the thought making me sad. Not because I was materialistic but because some of the pieces, the few I'd chosen myself, I really had liked.

Gabe glanced at his brother. "Didn't you say you were off at eleven? I thought we'd go check out the club I'm thinking of taking over."

"Are you really looking for a new club? Or is this trip an excuse to find some new woman to warm your bed?"

*His sibling doesn't pull punches*, I thought, glancing away, not wanting Gabe to see my reaction to the thought of any female in his bed.

"I'm still with Naomi."

My stomach still twisted uncomfortably.

His brother frowned. "She's a bitch."

I cleared my throat, unwilling to sit here a minute longer and listen to details of Gabe's love life. "Hello? Prisoner still here!" I reminded them with a wave of my free hand.

Gabe grinned at me.

I looked away, not wanting to acknowledge the utter rush of pleasure that small gesture brought me.

"What's she in for?" he asked his brother.

"Grand theft auto, but her boyfriend dropped the charges."

Gabe swore under his breath. "That son of a bitch had you arrested?"

I latched onto the latter part of Officer Dare's statement. "Lance dropped the charges?" Relief swamped me, and if I'd been standing, my knees might have given out.

"Charges dropped," the cop restated. "As long as you agree to relinquish the car."

My head whipped up. "That bastard." He was still trying to control me. He knew I'd left with next to nothing, yet he still had to strip me of the one thing he knew I loved. Realistically, however, since I couldn't afford to park my baby in the city, Lance had done me a favor.

"Deal," I said to Gabe's brother. "He can have the car."

"I wasn't negotiating," the cop said.

"Decklan." Gabe's tone held a definite warning.

I didn't need or want Gabe going to bat for me, and I ignored his hot—and I do mean hot—stare.

"Release me?" I jangled my chain.

Decklan—I now knew my jailer's name—nodded. "Your boyfriend said he'd come down to get you so you two could talk out this . . . misunderstanding. In which case maybe you can keep the automobile." He glanced at his watch. "He'll be here in about thirty minutes, give or take."

"Oh, hell no." I wasn't going anywhere with Lance, and I certainly didn't want the confrontation sure to come if he showed up. I jangled my cuffed wrist, suddenly desperate to escape. I had to get out of here *now*, and I needed a head start.

"Decklan! Unlock the damned cuffs," Gabe barked at his brother in a baritone that ironically settled me.

His officer brother, however, jumped to do his bidding.

I shook out my hand and glanced down. A red stripe bruised my skin, and I rubbed my sore wrist.

Gabe's gaze followed my every movement, his eyes darkening once more. With a low growl, he lifted my hand and stroked my marked flesh with his strong, tanned fingers. A sudden vision of him gripping me harder, pulling me roughly against him, grinding his muscular body into mine took form, and I trembled, aroused by his tone, his sensual touch, and my torturous thoughts.

"Are you okay?" Gabe asked gruffly.

His voice returned me to my current location and predicament. "Yes. Fine."

An intimate smile curved his lips, and I would swear he knew exactly how hot he'd made me, how wet.

Shaken by the thought and my impending reality, I grabbed my sweat shirt from the chair. "I'm free to go?" I asked, pulling on the light jacket.

"You are," his brother said. "Stay out of trouble, Miss Masters."

*I will*, I thought, *once I escape your brother*. I held out my hand, and Decklan handed me back my money.

"Thanks," I said and winced.

What was next? Gratitude for arresting me?

At least I hadn't gotten as far as the booking process and mug shot. I ran a hand through my wild curls, suddenly aware of how I might look.

"See you guys around," I said on a wave and a forced laugh.

"Wait!" Gabriel's deep pitch almost had me melting toward him again.

"What?"

"Do you have someplace to go?" he asked, too kind for me not to be embarrassed, and I refused to look him in the eye.

"I'll be fine."

"Isabelle—" Gabe's voice deepened.

"Oh no," his brother said. "Absolutely not."

"Shut up, Decklan."

I narrowed my eyes, wondering what conclusion the cop had arrived at that I wasn't privy to. My gaze swung back to Gabe, who merely nodded at his sibling, as if all had been decided.

"You'll come home with me," Gabe said, his tone definitive.

"What?" I hadn't seen that coming, nor could I begin to process the words.

He braced one hand on the wall beside his brother's desk. "You'll come home with me. I have plenty of room, and you can stay till you get back on your feet." His words sounded confident, sure, and obviously made sense, at least to him.

Panic spiraled through me at the thought of going from one controlling man to another.

"Are you insane?" Decklan asked. Loudly.

I nodded, agreeing with him. "Listen to your brother. I'm not going anywhere with you. You're practically a stranger."

Gabe frowned at that comment.

"And she's a stray," Decklan added.

"Hey!" I turned to him and scowled. "That's just insulting."

"You have a thing for strays," Decklan said to Gabe, ignoring me. Giving me more reason than just my arrest to dislike Officer Decklan Dare.

"Shut the fuck up," Gabe muttered, his jaw set as he glared at his brother.

Decklan had hit a hot button, I noted and wondered who the stray woman was to Gabe. What she'd meant to him.

I couldn't afford to find out. "It's been interesting," I said on a rush. "Later, boys."

And while the two brothers remained locked in a silent, combative stare, I turned and strode out of the station house without looking back.

Get *Dare to Surrender* now at your
local bookstore or buy online!

# ABOUT THE AUTHOR

Carly Phillips is the *New York Times* and *USA Today* bestselling author of more than fifty sexy contemporary romance novels featuring hot men, strong women, and the emotionally compelling stories her readers have come to expect and love. Carly's career spans over a decade and a half with various New York publishing houses, and she is now an indie author who runs her own business and loves every exciting minute of her publishing journey. Carly is  happily married to her college sweetheart and is the mother of two nearly adult daughters and three crazy dogs (two wheaten terriers and one mutant Havanese) who star on her Facebook fan page and website. Carly loves social media and is always around to interact with her readers. You can find out more about Carly at www.carlyphillips.com.

# Carly's Booklist by Series

**Dare to Love Series**
Book 1: *Dare to Love* (Ian & Riley)
Book 2: *Dare to Desire*
(Alex & Madison)
Book 3: *Dare to Touch*
(Olivia & Dylan)
Book 4: *Dare to Hold* (Scott & Meg)
Book 5: *Dare to Rock* (Avery & Grey)
Book 6: *Dare to Take* (Tyler & Ella)

**NY Dares Series**
Book 1: *Dare to Surrender*
(Gabe & Isabelle)
Book 2: *Dare to Submit*
(Decklan & Amanda)
Book 3: *Dare to Seduce*
(Max & Lucy)

*The NY Dares books are
more erotic/hotter books.

**Serendipity Series**
*Serendipity*
*Destiny*
*Karma*

**Serendipity's Finest Series**
*Perfect Fit*
*Perfect Fling*
*Perfect Together*

**Serendipity Novellas**
*Fated*
*Hot Summer Nights*
(Perfect Stranger)

**Bachelor Blog Series**
*Kiss Me If You Can*
*Love Me If You Dare*

**Lucky Series**
*Lucky Charm*
*Lucky Streak*
*Lucky Break*

**Ty and Hunter Series**
*Cross My Heart*
*Sealed with a Kiss*

**Hot Zone Series**
*Hot Stuff*
*Hot Number*
*Hot Item*
*Hot Property*

**Costas Sisters Series**
*Summer Lovin'*
*Under the Boardwalk*

**Chandler Brothers Series**
*The Bachelor*
*The Playboy*
*The Heartbreaker*

**Stand-Alone Titles**
*Brazen*
*Seduce Me*
*Secret Fantasy*
*The Right Choice*
*Suddenly Love*
*Perfect Partners*
*Unexpected Chances*
*Worthy of Love*

# Keep up with Carly and her upcoming books:

Website:
www.carlyphillips.com

Sign up for blog and website updates:
www.carlyphillips.com/category/blog/

Sign up for Carly's newsletter:
www.carlyphillips.com/newsletter-sign-up

Carly on Facebook:
www.facebook.com/CarlyPhillipsFanPage

Carly on Twitter:
www.twitter.com/carlyphillips

Hang out at Carly's Corner—hot guys & giveaways!
smarturl.it/CarlysCornerFB

CPSIA information can be obtained
at www.ICGtesting.com
Printed in the USA
LVOW03s0037190517
534935LV00001B/1/P